Cracked
Classics

Crack open all the books in

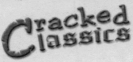

Around the World in Eighty Days

What a Trip!

By Tony Abbott

Hyperion
New York

Printed in the United States of America
First Edition
1 3 5 7 9 10 8 6 4 2
This book is set in 11.5-pt. Cheltenham.

ISBN 0-7868-1326-1
Visit www.volobooks.com

Cracked Classics

Chapter 1

"Everyone ready for our field trip?" my English teacher, Mr. Wexler, chirped. "All right, then. Let's go!"

"This is a field trip?" a voice hissed in my ear. "I don't call this a field trip. Devin, do you call this a field trip? Because, if you ask me, I don't call this a field trip!"

I'm Devin Bundy. The person hissing in my ear was my-very-best-friend-despite-the-fact-that-she's-a-girl, Frankie Lang. We're in the sixth grade at Palmdale Middle School, and at the moment we were following Mr. Wexler and the rest of our class on a field trip.

Down the hall and around the corner.

To the school library.

"This is definitely stretching the definition of field trip," I replied to Frankie as we tramped past the main office. "I see no fields, because we are totally inside. And I usually reserve the word 'trip' for something that involves a bus with a bathroom. But then, I didn't hear Mr. Wexler even talking about a trip because I was working on another project."

Frankie frowned at me. "What other project?"

"A dream I was having. I dreamed that I was sleeping in class and having a dream about sleeping in class."

She nodded. "Devin, you've had that dream before."

"It's one of my favorites," I said.

Now, there's something you need to know about Frankie and me. People say that the only way to succeed in life is to develop your talents. So we have.

Frankie is really amazing at staring into space.

My own specialty is dozing in class.

Hey, it's what we do well.

What we don't do well is read. We test pretty low on the whole book-reading thing. Of course, Mr. Wexler wants to help us do better. He's sure we have great potential.

"Everyone—here we are!" Mr. Wexler said excitedly as we reached the library entrance.

Frankie was so disappointed, her hair drooped.

"I bet Mrs. Figglehopper is behind this whole

field-trip thing," she said. "She'll probably pop out from behind a book and make us read something!"

Mrs. Figglehopper is the not-too-ordinary librarian of Palmdale Middle School. She always wears long, flowery dresses. Her gray hair is tied up in a tight knob at the back of her head. And she's severely nutty about old books. You know the kind of books I mean. People call them classics.

Mrs. Figglehopper and Mr. Wexler are like the one-two punch of reading. He assigns fat old books, and her library has loads of copies of them.

But that isn't the only thing about our teacher and our librarian. Because of stuff we've done, and some stuff we haven't done, Mr. Wexler has sentenced us to work in Mrs. Figglehopper's library workroom a couple of times.

And let me tell you something. The weirdest things happen in that library workroom.

As we stood outside the library, Frankie and I glanced at each other. I could tell from the look in her eye that we were both remembering some of those weird things.

"Zapper gates," whispered Frankie.

"Zapper gates," I whispered back to her.

The zapper gates are what Mrs. Figglehopper calls an old set of security gates that she keeps in the workroom. They're the kind of gates that are supposed to go *zzzt-zzzt!* when you take a book through them that hasn't been checked out right.

The librarian has told us, like, a thousand times that those gates are broken and that someday she'll get them repaired to work right again.

Except that the gates aren't exactly broken.

One day, Frankie and I found out that those gates can sizzle and fizzle and spark and flicker and drop you right into a book.

Yes! Into a book! Right there with all the characters and places and story and everything!

The first time it happened, Frankie and I were fighting over a book. It fell through the gates, light exploded everywhere, and the wall behind the gates cracked open.

When we went through, we ended up right smack at the beginning of the book. Our only way home was to follow the characters all the way to the end of the story.

We almost didn't believe it had actually happened. Except that we got our best grades ever when we got tested on the books we fell into. And you can't take our grades away. They're part of our permanent record.

Mr. Wexler snapped his fingers, said, "Enter!" and we pushed through the library's double doors into the main room. It was filled with study carrels and tables and lots and lots of bookshelves, each one jammed with—guess what?—books.

I felt an uncontrollable urge to yawn.

"Devin," said Mr. Wexler, "if you can get your head out of that *fog* you're in, you might learn something fun!"

I stifled the yawn, but I knew it would come back.

"Good," said our teacher. "Mrs. Figglehopper has prepared for us a special display of beautiful books from many different countries around the world—England, India, China, Japan, France . . . ah!"

Just as my yawn made a return visit, Mr. Wexler's eyes lit up with excitement. He scampered over to a small display in the center of the room.

On the display were two things: a book and a watch. The book had a crusty green cover and looked old. The watch was one of those ancient pocket types that people used to have before they invented wrists or something. Right now, the top of the watch was flipped open, but the watch wasn't ticking.

"Class, this great classic adventure is one of the centerpieces of the display," Mr. Wexler said, picking up the book carefully. "It is called *Around the World in Eighty Days*. It's a fabulous story published in 1873 by the French author Jules Verne. Few of us get to go on a journey around the world, but we can get a sense of what it's like by reading this classic book."

"Why is there a watch on display, too?" I asked.

"Good question," said Mr. Wexler. "To find out the answer, all you have to do is . . ."

"What?" said Frankie.

"Read the book!"

"Not fair," I grumbled.

Mr. Wexler put the book down. "Now, please follow me. We have only about an hour and twenty minutes—oh! That's funny! Eighty minutes. Let's take our tour around the world of books in eighty minutes! Eighty days, eighty minutes? Get it?"

We got it. It wasn't all that amazing.

"And . . . here we go!" he said. He marched off to the first display table. The other kids followed him.

The pain was too much for my head. I turned to my friend. "Eighty whole minutes? I can't do booky things for that long. My head starts to explode. I say we head straight for the food."

"What food?" asked Frankie.

I pointed to a table outside the workroom in the corner. On it was a big pink box. "Doughnuts, my friend, doughnuts. My nose can spot them a mile away."

Frankie grinned, glanced at Mr. Wexler, then stepped slyly up to the book display. "Devin, I'll pretend to examine this old busted watch while you pretend to read this old book. With Mr. Wexler

6

thinking we're working, we'll take our own little field trip to Doughnutville."

"Frankie, I love how you think. Let's do it!"

I picked up the book and held it as if I were reading. Frankie took the watch, and pretended to be amazed at the cool oldness of it. We headed for the pink box.

When we got near, we heard low voices coming from the workroom. Peeking in, we saw Mrs. Figglehopper and a guy in blue overalls standing in front of the zapper gates.

"What's going on?" Frankie asked.

"Mrs. F and some work guy," I whispered.

Then, before our shocked eyeballs, the work guy pulled a screwdriver from his tool belt, knelt down, and began to take the zapper gates apart!

Chapter 2

Frankie gasped. "Who is he, and what is he doing?"

"He's wrecking our zapper gates!" I hissed. "Frankie, we owe our only good grades to those gates! Can we let him do this?"

"Shhh," she said. "Mrs. Figglehopper is saying something—"

We snuck through the open door, hid behind a crowded bookshelf, and listened closely.

"There's something wrong with the gates," Mrs. Figglehopper said. She placed a sheet of blue paper on the table next to the guy. "It's all in the work order."

"I'll check them out right away," he said. "Give me about an hour and twenty minutes. I'll be done then."

She glanced at the clock on the wall. "Good.

Eighty minutes is perfect," she said. Giving a cheery nod to the guy, she left the room.

I nudged Frankie. "She never even saw us—"

But Frankie was watching the repairman unscrew a panel on the side of one gate. He tugged out a bunch of colored wires and began to untangle them.

Frankie clutched my arm tightly. "Devin, he's going to wreck the gates forever. That means no more dropping into books. We need to stop this guy—"

Suddenly, my head lit up with an idea. "If I know work guys, he won't be able to resist the call of the cruller." Stepping out from behind the shelf, I walked over to him. "Um, excuse me, sir?"

The guy didn't look up. "Yeah?"

"I know you're busy, but did you know there's a box of doughnuts just outside this room?"

He stopped working. "Powdered?"

"Oh, yes. Lots of them. Right outside this door."

Plink! His screwdriver hit the floor. *Fwit!* He shot out of the room. *Slam!* Frankie shut the door behind him.

We scrambled over and read the blue work order.

"'Complete overhaul?'" Frankie read with a gasp. "'Something funny going on? Fix blue light? Short circuits! Rewiring!' Devin, according to this, the repair guy is going to turn our incredible zapper gates into nothing more than a set of dumb old security gates!"

"He'll mess up the gates forever!" I said. "No more falling into books. No more good grades. All those books we'll have to read! What should we do?"

"You hide the work order!" she said.

"And you hide the tools!" I said.

But the moment I reached for the work order was the same moment Frankie reached for the tools. We collided, and the book, the special copy of *Around the World in Eighty Days* that I had been holding, went flying out of my hand. And right between the zapper gates.

KKKKK! The whole room lit up like fireworks. A sizzling, crackling, flaming burst of blue light shot out from between the gates and bounced around the room.

"I can't believe it's happening again!" cried Frankie.

"It's different this time!" I said. "The guy already messed with the wires. The gates are acting funny. We shouldn't go near them—"

"Too late," she said. "Something's—got—me!"

Even as we tried to back away, the zapper gates sparked more wildly and hummed more loudly, and we found ourselves being pulled toward them.

"What's going on?" Frankie cried, holding on to the file cabinet.

It was only too clear what was going on.

10

Frankie and I were being sucked into the blue light coming from the crack in the wall! It pulled and yanked and dragged us toward it. The light flooded over us. It flooded *through* us, too.

"I'm electric!" I cried, almost entirely blue now.

"And . . . I'm . . . I'm . . ." cried Frankie.

Everything went dark. And there were no more bookshelves. No more zapper gates. No more workroom. No more library.

Frankie and I found ourselves outside rolling over and over a bunch of knobby cobblestones on some old street somewhere.

We bounced and tumbled and tumbled and bounced—"Ouch! Oof! Hey!"—until we stopped at the feet of a little man in a tight, little suit.

He bowed sharply to us.

"Good day!" he chirped. "Are you Fogg?"

Chapter 3

He was a short guy with a smudgy, thin mustache and a bright, cheery look in his eye. But what he said didn't make a whole lot of sense.

"Are you Fogg?" he repeated, smiling politely.

"Fog?" said Frankie. "Sometimes Mr. Wexler says Devin's brain is in a fog—"

The man shook his head vigorously. "No, no. I mean Phileas Fogg. I am the new servant of Mr. Phileas Fogg whose house is at Number Seven, Saville Row! Passepartout is my name. It is pronounced Pass—par—too! I am French, from France. In fact, I am a Parisian from Paris."

"I'm a Devin," I told him. "This is a Frankie. We're

Palmdale Middle Schoolians from Palmdale Middle School. It's a long way from here."

"By the way," said Frankie, "where is *here*?"

"London, of course!" the man replied.

"That's England, right?" I said.

"Of course!"

"Dude," I said to Frankie. "I got one right."

Frankie made a face at me. "Excuse him, Passepartout, but what year is it?"

"Eighteen hundred and seventy-two!" he said brightly. "Now, if you will be so good as to help me find Mr. Fogg's house, I would thank you."

Frankie and I both shrugged at each other. There was no denying it. We had landed in a book again. The same book that was sitting on the sidewalk in front of me. *Around the World in Eighty Days*. I picked it up and flipped to the first page. "Here we go again," I said.

"Okay, Passepartout," said Frankie. "Let's go."

"Good," he said, heading down the street. "I cannot be late. The agency that hired me has told me that Mr. Fogg is very punctual, very exact. He fired his last servant because he heated Mr. Fogg's shaving water two degrees lower than requested! And shaving water to an Englishman such as Mr. Fogg is a very serious matter!"

Horses and carriages *clip-clop*ped by us.

Everyone was wearing old-fashioned clothes, the men in suits and women in long dresses and hats. Lots of umbrellas.

Finally, we turned the corner onto a wide street of brick and stone houses. The sign said SAVILLE ROW.

"Mr. Fogg, they say, is very rich," Passepartout went on. "He spends much of his time playing cards with his friends at the Reform Club, a very famous club of the richest gentlemen in London! This is the sort of person my new master is!"

"Sounds a little dull," said Frankie.

"I want dull!" said Passepartout. "After spending many years as a circus juggler and acrobat, bicycle racer, and street singer, I am looking to work for a quiet man! I yearn for rest."

"I love to rest!" I said. "It's my specialty, in fact."

"And what restful activities do you prefer?" asked Passepartout.

"English class," I said. "It's a good place to sleep."

"Well, here we are," said Frankie, pointing to a green door with a gold knocker on it.

"Let's knock," said Passepartout. "How do I look?"

"Cool," I said.

"I do not feel cool," he said. "I feel very nervous!"

Using the knocker, Passepartout announced that we were there. A moment later, the door opened and there stood a well-dressed man. He was tall and thin, and had a neat, short beard. He was about the age of my dad, maybe a tiny bit older.

The guy had no wrinkles anywhere on his clothes. He looked like one of those store dummies, except that his eyes looked smart, and he obviously had a lot going on inside his dome.

"I am Phileas Fogg," he stated.

"Good day, sir!" said Passepartout. "I am—"

Mr. Fogg held up his hand abruptly. "What is the proper temperature for shaving water?"

"Man!" Frankie whispered to me. "A quiz already?"

Passepartout blinked. "Eighty-six degrees."

"Correct," said Phileas Fogg. "You may enter."

He waved his hand and we passed through into the entrance hall of a very quiet and very neat house.

"I'm Frankie," said Frankie going in. "This is Devin."

Taking us into his living room, Mr. Fogg said, "I am exact. I am settled. I am quiet. My life is one of unbroken regularity. I have my routines. I wake every morning at precisely eight o'clock."

Passepartout nodded sharply. "Yes, Mr. Fogg."

"I have toast at twenty-three minutes past eight."

"Yes, Mr. Fogg."

"I shave at thirty-seven minutes past eight."

"Yes, Mr. Fogg."

"I do not like turbulence in my household. Is this understood?"

"Yes, Mr. Fogg!"

"Good," the man said. He pulled a watch from his pocket. "What time do you have?"

"Twenty-two minutes past eleven," said Passepartout.

"You are four minutes slow," Fogg said.

"My watch is set on Paris time," said Passepartout.

"You are in London now," said Mr. Fogg.

"Then I shall change to London time!" said Passepartout. He twisted a knob on his watch. "There."

"Good," said Fogg. "From this moment, twenty-six minutes after eleven A.M., Wednesday, October second, you are my servant."

"Thank you, sir!" said Passepartout. He leaned forward as if he were going to hug Mr. Fogg, but his new master swiftly put up his hand to stop him.

"Now, Passepartout," he said, "there are exactly one thousand one hundred fifty-one steps from my door to the door of the Reform Club, and I have exactly three minutes and forty-two seconds in which to traverse that distance. Therefore, I must now leave."

Without another word, Phileas Fogg took his hat in his hand, put it on his head, and slipped through the front door, closed it behind him, and was gone.

"Wow," I said. "He's very . . . very . . ."

"I know!" said Frankie, peeking out a front window.

As Fogg left the house and crossed the street, an out-of-control carriage dragged by two wild horses shot right by him. Fogg kept walking at the same pace.

"That carriage almost ran him down!" I said.

"He didn't even notice," said Frankie.

"The man is a machine!" said Passepartout.

"A robot," said Frankie.

"A fast robot!" I said, as we watched Phileas Fogg walk quickly down the street.

Chapter 4

While Passepartout wandered off to explore Mr. Fogg's house, Frankie took the book from me.

"We need to follow Fogg," she said after reading a couple of pages. "He's where the action is now."

"Good idea," I said. "Bring the book."

"And the watch," said Frankie, holding up the old watch. "I guess I slipped it in my pocket by mistake."

"Do you think Mrs. Figglehopper will be mad that we borrowed her stuff?"

Frankie shook her head. "Nah, we'll be back in no time."

I remembered how the work guy was messing with the wires. I wondered if this was going to be like our other adventures or not.

Soon after heading out the door, we caught up with Mr. Fogg. He was walking along a London street, when he suddenly turned and climbed a set of stairs.

"One thousand one hundred fifty . . . one thousand one hundred fifty-one!" he said. Then he glanced at his watch. "At the Reform Club at exactly eleven-thirty."

He stepped up to the door.

"Why do you count your steps?" Frankie asked him.

"The information may be useful one day," he replied.

"In case someone gives you a test?" I asked.

"Life is a test," said Fogg. "Let us enter."

Inside the Reform Club, the noise of the street died away. All the horses *clip-clop*ping, and carts and carriages and delivery wagons creaking, and people talking and walking and yelling, just stopped.

An old, bent-over little man met us at the door. "Your newspaper, Mr. Fogg," he said. "The news today is about a robbery at the Bank of England, sir."

"Indeed," said Mr. Fogg. He took the paper and entered a big quiet room.

Frankie nudged me. "This place is like a—"

"I know," I whispered. "A library!"

The rooms were paneled with dark wood. Bookcases reached from floor to ceiling. As soon as I

19

saw them I started to feel sleepy, just like in our own library. And I wasn't the only one. The loudest thing in the whole place was the snoring of a couple of really ancient dudes in deep leather chairs in the back.

Right away, I noticed a table laid out with munchies. While Fogg went straight to a table to play cards with his friends, I made an emergency pit stop at the food table and began stuffing myself with a bunch of tasty crackers. *Crunch . . . crunch.*

"Thief!" said one of the men at Fogg's table.

I quickly swallowed the rest of my crackers. "I'm innocent!" I proclaimed. "I just ate two. Well, three. Okay, five. But some of the six were broken, which is why I only had eight of them. Nine!"

"Devin, calm down!" said Frankie, with a frown. "If you'd stop crunching and maybe pay attention, you'd know they're talking about the *other* robbery."

I looked at the men with Fogg. It was true. They were all buzzing about the same thing, and it wasn't me.

"A thief stole fifty-five thousand pounds from the Bank of England last night, Fogg!" said one of the men.

Frankie and I went over to the old-guy table.

"Indeed, I heard," said Fogg. "Disgraceful."

I raised my hand. "How could anyone steal something that heavy?" I asked. "If there are two thousand pounds in a ton, then fifty-five thousand pounds is—"

Mr. Fogg set down his cards and turned to us. "The standard denomination of English currency is called a pound, just as American money is made up of dollars."

"Oh, I get it," I said. "Sorry."

"Not at all," said Fogg politely. "For you bring up an interesting point. Fifty-five thousand pounds, even in paper bills, makes a very heavy load. The robber must be very clever to have gotten away with it. The newspaper states that he may even be a gentleman."

The other guys made noises at this.

"Detectives have gone off around the world searching for the fellow," one growled as he snapped a card onto the table. "There is a large reward for his capture."

"But of course, the world is such a big place, he could hide anywhere," said another.

Fogg played a card. "The world is not so large."

"I rather agree," said the man to his left. "They say you can go round the globe in three months or so."

"In eighty days," said Fogg, playing another card.

I thought about that. "That's slow," I said to Frankie. "With jets, it probably only takes a couple days."

Frankie shook her head. "Jets haven't been invented yet. Planes, neither. It's 1872, remember?"

"Ouch," I said. "Cruel ancient world."

"Eighty days," Fogg repeated. "Indeed, today's newspaper even gives an estimate of the traveling time."

He flipped open the paper to the travel section and showed everyone the timetable.

From London to Suez, by rail and steamboat . . . . . . 7 days

From Suez to Bombay, India, by steamer . . . . 13 days

From Bombay to Calcutta, by rail . . . . 3 days

From Calcutta to Hong Kong, by steamer . . . . 13 days

From Hong Kong to Yokohama, by steamer . . . . 6 days

From Yokohama to San Francisco, by steamer . . . . 22 days

From San Francisco to New York, by rail . . . . 7 days

From New York to London, by steamer and rail . . . . 9 days

Total: 80 days

One of the gentleman laughed. "Yes, eighty days! But that doesn't take into account bad weather, shipwrecks, railway accidents, missed connections, and the thousand other mishaps that can happen in faraway countries!"

"All included," said Fogg.

Another of the men made a gargling noise. "On paper it's one thing, Fogg. But I'd like to see you actually do it in eighty days—"

Fogg set his cards down and looked at the man. "I

have in my bank account twenty thousand pounds. I will wager that it can be done, and I will prove it by going myself."

The other men put down their cards. They looked as if they would just keel over and hit the floor.

"You're not serious, Fogg," murmured one.

Phileas Fogg stood up from the table. "An Englishman never jokes about a wager. Gentlemen, I will bet twenty thousand pounds against anyone who wishes that I can make the tour of the world in eighty days or less. That is, in nineteen hundred twenty hours, or one hundred fifteen thousand, two hundred minutes. Do you accept?"

The other men stood up. One by one, they stared at him, then at one another. "Fogg, it's a deal!" they cried.

It was then that I realized something. I pulled Frankie off a little. "You know what this means? If this happens, if Fogg goes on this trip, and that's what the book is really about, we'll have to go all the way around the world with him to get to the end of this book!"

My friend looked at me. Her face went pale. "Around the world? That's a lot farther than we've gone before."

"Now, gentlemen," Fogg was saying, "a train leaves for the coast at a quarter before nine this evening—"

Frankie looked at Mr. Fogg. "Um . . . I think we have to come, too."

Mr. Fogg made a face that looked as if he might be smiling, but it was hard to tell. "As you wish. So, gentlemen, my new friends here, my servant, and I will be on tonight's train."

"Tonight?" blustered one of the men.

Fogg made a brief nod and pulled from his pocket a small notebook. "Today is Wednesday, October second. Therefore, we are due back in this very room of the Reform Club on Saturday, December twenty-first, at a quarter before nine P.M. If we are not, I lose the wager and you men are twenty thousand pounds richer. Agreed?"

"Agreed!" the men chimed together.

Frankie blinked. "So we're going around the world?"

"Around the world," said Fogg.

I gulped. "Now that's what I call a field trip!"

Chapter 5

"Passepartout isn't going to like it," Frankie said as we strode back every single one of the one thousand one hundred fifty-one steps to Mr. Fogg's place. "He was all about having a peaceful life serving tea and toast and keeping the water at the right temperature."

Fogg seemed to understand what Frankie meant, then said, "We shall be leaving in twenty-two minutes."

With that, the man disappeared into his room.

When Frankie and I burst into the little Frenchman's room, he was in his pajamas and slippers, reading quietly in a chair. We had to break it to him about what we were doing and how it had happened.

"Aye-yi-yiiii!" he yelped. "Around the world! Around the world? But we are not packed—"

Fogg stepped in at that moment, holding a giant carpetbag. "We will not pack. We shall buy what we need along the way."

"What, no carry-on luggage?" I said.

"But I wanted rest! Quiet! Peace!" Passepartout said.

"You can rest in quiet peace eighty days from now when we are back in London," said Fogg, "for I intend to win this wager."

He flew past us, went to his safe, and took out a chubby wad of money and stuffed it in the bag. Then he turned, checked his watch, smiled slightly, and said, "We're off."

Nineteen minutes later, we were at a big train station in London and rushing after Fogg, who was calmly striding toward a train that was blasting out steam and already starting to roll down the tracks.

The next thing that happened was strange.

Just as Mr. Fogg was about to hop onto the train, he spotted a poor woman holding a small child in her arms, huddled against the station wall.

Without a word, Fogg trotted over and gave her a giant silver coin. "Here, my good woman," he said. "I'm glad I met you!"

Then he shot back and hopped onto the moving train.

"Ah, my master," whispered Passepartout, his eyes twinkling. "Perhaps he is not such a robot. . . ."

A moment later, the train blasted out of the station and we were chugging toward the coast of England.

"Do you believe this?" I said when we settled into our seats. "We're going around the world. I mean, I know about the world pretty well from TV, but the real thing is supposed to be even better!"

Frankie looked out the window at the countryside whizzing by. "I guess if we had to drop into a book, this isn't a bad one. We'll see the sights at least. Hey, look."

She had pulled that old watch out of her pocket and was glancing at it. "It just started ticking again."

"You probably knocked something loose when we scurried for the train," said Passepartout. "And now, my new friends, prepare to see Paris, my beloved City of Light. It is just a few hours away. I guarantee you will love it!"

But by the time we got to the coast of England and took a boat to France and then another train straight to Paris, it was the middle of the night. We were in the train station the whole time, and we left Paris in twenty minutes, anyway.

Passepartout pressed his nose up against the window as we left the Paris station. "Oh, dear, dear. This trip around the world is fast. Good-bye, Paris!"

"What's next?" I asked.

"Rome," said Frankie, peeking into the book. "Which I think is the Paris of Italy. Where they make all that Italian food. It's the official home of the meatball—"

"What a coincidence!" I said. "I love meatballs! And most other types of food."

But we didn't get any meatballs or anything.

Whoosh! A bunch of lights flashed by the window.

"What was that?" I asked.

Passepartout sighed. "Rome."

"We're going fast, all right," said Frankie as the train chugged and rattled through the countryside. "But we're not exactly seeing the world."

I chuckled. "Not stopping anywhere does solve the whole problem of how to pack the souvenirs!"

Soon it was Saturday, which from the book we realized was the third day of our trip, and we were all the way down at the very bottom of Italy.

It was there, in a city named Brindisi (Brin-DEE-zee, according to Passepartout), that we got onto a steamer called the *Mongolia*.

"The *Mongolia* will take us from Italy across the Mediterranean Sea, through the Suez Canal to India," Mr. Fogg said when we tumbled out of the train and zipped over to the Brindisi harbor.

He was right.

For the next four days we steamed across the blue Mediterranean. Frankie and I were getting tired reading page after page, so it felt good when we arrived on the south shore of that big sea for our first real stop.

"Suez!" called out one of the ship guys.

"Finally, some sight-seeing," said Frankie.

Another bunch of ship guys slid a ramp out from the steamer to the dock where we were stopping to refuel.

Together with Passepartout, Mr. Fogg went straight to the office where they stamp passports, so he could prove to his friends in London that he'd been there.

"According to the book," I said, as Frankie and I stepped down the plank to the dock, "Suez is a port in Egypt. Egypt is the home of the pyramids. I love those things. I always wanted to climb to the top, then slide down—what's the matter?"

Frankie pointed to two men pacing the dock below. One was like an official British man in a blue uniform.

The other guy was small and wore a wrinkled suit that had probably been white in the age of the pyramids.

"Check him out," said Frankie.

"I'm checking," I said.

The man's beady little eyes darted from one passenger to the next. He also had a strange mustache under his nose. It was all gunked up with wax, and the ends were twisted into two points. He tried not to attract any attention, but he jumped when he saw Mr. Fogg.

"It's like he knows Mr. Fogg or something," I said. "Could he be another character in the story?"

"Check the book."

I flipped it open. "Okay, here we are in Suez on day seven of our trip. We're on the dock . . . wait . . . sorry, the pages are getting too blurry to read."

This is another thing that happens in the books we get dropped into. If the words get blurry, it means we're getting too far ahead in the story, and we have to stop reading. We're not supposed to jump ahead to stuff that hasn't happened yet—just like you shouldn't skip anything when you actually read a book.

"Well," I said, closing the book, "if he is a character, he's a suspicious one. We should find out what he's up to . . . but how . . . ?"

Suddenly Frankie grinned. "Hey, Devin, are you thinking what I'm thinking?"

"Where to find cheeseburgers at this time of day?"

"No, I'm thinking we go into sneaky mode and listen in on the dude's conversation."

I grinned. "You think good, Frankie. Entering sneaky mode . . . now!"

We crept up behind the guys pacing the dock and hid behind a carriage hitched to a horse. The man in the blue uniform was talking. "Are you certain?"

"I tell you," replied the mustache man, "I've found him. And a good job I've done of it, too. I searched the steamer's list of passengers, and found my man. Now I need you to issue me a warrant for his arrest."

Frankie tugged my robe. "The guy in white is some kind of detective. Shhh . . ."

"I tell you," said the detective, "the bank robber is right on this ship. Mr. Fogg is our bank robber!"

I nearly exploded. "What?"

"I'm sure of it," the detective went on. "Phileas Fogg, gentleman of London, has stolen fifty-five thousand pounds from the Bank of England!"

Chapter 6

Frankie and I turned to each other and gasped.

"A police detective!" she hissed. "And he thinks Phileas Fogg is the guy who robbed the Bank of England!"

"So *that's* why we got so much information about the robbery back at Fogg's club in London," I said. "It didn't really seem like part of the story. But now it all makes sense. Wait, there's more. Shhh!"

"But, Detective Fix," the officer in blue was saying, "Phileas Fogg appears an honest man and a gentleman."

"Great robbers always resemble honest folks," said the detective. "It's easy for gentlemen to make their escape that way. But I can't arrest him outside

England unless he's in an English colony, such as Egypt. And I can't do it without an arrest warrant."

The other man pointed down the dock. "Here comes his servant now."

"Good. I shall interrogate him!" said Detective Fix. He whirled around quickly and purposely bumped into Passepartout on the dock.

"Oh, sir, I beg your pardon," said the detective, twirling the ends of his mustache. "Are you traveling with Mr. Phileas Fogg?"

"Why, sir, yes I am!" said Passepartout, giving a bow.

"And where is your master traveling to?"

The servant chuckled to himself. "Why, Mr. Fogg is going around the world. In eighty days! Our next stop is Bombay, India! After that China, then Japan!"

Fix nodded at this information. "Is he rich, then?"

"He carries a great deal of money," said Passepartout.

"Oh, man!" I whispered. "Don't tell him that!"

"A great deal of money, eh? Does he, really?" Fix's eyes lit up. "Well, perhaps I'll meet him on board. Because I'll be going to Bombay also."

Then the detective wandered away, practically twisting his mustache ends right off.

"I knew that mustache was up to no good," said Frankie. "We need to tell Passepartout the truth."

Clack! Clack! The carriage suddenly rode away and there we were, huddled on the dock like a couple of scared monkeys.

"Ah, Frankie and Devin!" said Passepartout. "Are you quite all right?"

"We're okay," I said. "But Mr. Fogg may not be. That man you were talking to is a police detective. And he thinks Mr. Fogg is the one who robbed the Bank of England—"

"I don't understand a word you're saying," said Passepartout. "Do you often say silly things?"

"Like what, for instance?" asked Frankie.

"Like . . . blah, blah, mumble, mumble? By the way, Fix seems like a friendly, delightful fellow, doesn't he?"

We stared at him. Just then, the ship's whistle blew loudly. It meant that the *Mongolia* was ready to leave.

As all three of us made our way to the plank, Frankie turned to me and whispered. "We've had this problem before. You try to tell a character something that they're not supposed to know yet, and it's all blah, blah, mumble, mumble to them. It makes you sound like an idiot."

"Even more than usual," I groaned. "But that's not the worst part. What if Detective Fix tries to stop Fogg?"

Suddenly, Frankie stopped cold. "Whoa, I just thought of something." She shoved her hand into her pocket and pulled out the old watch. "Oh, man!"

"What's the matter?"

"You said that according to the book, we're on the seventh day of the journey, right?"

"It says right here, seven days." I tapped the page.

"This strange old watch has gone exactly *seven minutes* since it started ticking again."

"The watch is ancient," I said. "It doesn't keep time."

"No!" Frankie said loudly. "Devin! It just hit me! The watch *does* keep time. But it's not the time here in the story. It's the time back in Palmdale. It's the eighty minutes of our trip at the library. It's the same eighty minutes that the repair guy told Mrs. Figglehopper he needed to fix the gates! You know what this means?"

Now, I was *trying* to understand what she was saying. I saw her lips moving and heard the words. It's just that this whole business about time was always tough for me. I'm personally always late for stuff.

I guess I looked like I wasn't getting it.

"It means," said Frankie, "that this watch is showing how much time we have left before that repair guy completely messes up our zapper gates. Usually, no time passes while we're in a book. But the guy fooled with the wires, so it's different now. If he fixes the gates before we get back, we'll be trapped here—forever!"

It was starting to dawn on me. "So you're saying if we're late, if this trip takes more than eighty days—"

"Eighty minutes on this watch," said Frankie.

"—not only will Fogg lose the bet but the zapper gates will get fixed and we'll be trapped here forever?"

"That's what I just said!"

"Which means—"

"We stay in 1872!"

"Where there are no—"

"Cheeseburgers or cable!"

"So then we've got to—"

"Stop Fix!"

"Before he—"

"Stops us!"

"Or even before!" I cried. "And we have only seventy-three minutes left to do it in!"

"Seventy-three days," said Fogg calmly as he passed by, striding up the plank. "Seventy-three days."

"You see!" whispered Frankie. "Minutes equal days!"

I shook my head. "This is so very confusing—"

"Come along!" said Passepartout. "They are serving lunch on the ship. And we cannot be late for lunch."

I grinned. "Now, *that* I understand!"

The whistle blew, and the *Mongolia* was ready to steam out of the Suez harbor on its way to Bombay. We ran with top speed back to the ship.

A moment later, we headed out to sea.

Chapter 7

While the *Mongolia* traveled down the Red Sea between Egypt and Arabia, Frankie and I strolled the deck, trying to get a handle on our problem.

"Let me get this straight," I said. "We have to finish going around the world before that techie at the library fixes the gates and closes our escape route, right?"

Frankie nodded. "Right."

"But Detective Fix is trying to stop Mr. Fogg's trip, so right now he's our biggest problem."

"Right," said Frankie. "And guess what?"

"What?"

"Here comes our biggest problem."

The guy with the twirly mustache climbed up the stairs from a lower deck and spotted us.

"He's so annoying," said Frankie. "I bet he's going to try to weasel some info about Mr. Fogg out of us."

"Is it bad to throw a book character off a ship?"

Frankie laughed. "Maybe we can just throw him off the scent. Here he comes."

The man twisted the ends of his mustache as he sauntered over. "You are friends of Mr. Fogg, aren't you?"

Before I could get a word out, Frankie went straight to the point. "Yes, we are . . . Detective Fix!"

"Detective?" He narrowed his eyes. "I'm sure I don't know what you mean! I work for the shipping company. Really, I do."

"Yeah, right," I said to myself. Then I had an idea. I pulled out the book and opened it. "Since you work for the shipping company, you probably know all about India, right?"

"Of course!" he said. "I, er, travel to India all the time."

"Well this book is about India," I said. Then, winking at Frankie, I said, "They say a great site to visit in India is a place called . . . Palmdale. What's it like?"

"Palmdale, eh?" Fix shifted his eyes nervously. "Oh, a beautiful place. Lovely place. Exotic. Full of enchantment, yes . . ."

"Could you be more specific?" asked Frankie, giving him a cold stare.

Fix looked away. "Well, Palmdale is full of palms, isn't it? And dales. It has several of those. Oh, yes, lovely palms and dales. Wait, what's that? Oh, I think I hear my name being called. I must be going. Good day!"

He scuttled off nervously.

"What a fibber!" I said. "He doesn't know India!"

"We'd better keep an eye on the guy."

"Or four eyes," I said. "Your two plus my two."

"You're so good at math. Come on, let's do lunch."

It was more of the same for the next few days, as the steamer finally left the Red Sea and launched out into the Indian Ocean. Waves, water, wetness, you know.

Then, on Sunday, October 20, at around two in the afternoon, the *Mongolia* arrived in the port of Bombay.

For the entire voyage, Mr. Fogg had played cards with an English soldier named Sir Francis Cromarty. Sir Francis was a nice old man who actually did know about India. I hoped he'd turn out to be a good character in this story.

When Mr. Fogg finally appeared on deck, carpet-bag in hand, having seen none of the voyage, he announced, "According to my calculations, we have arrived two days ahead of schedule. This is good news."

"Good news? This is wondrous news!" said Passepartout, hanging over the railing and gazing at the giant city that spread out before us. "Bombay! India! I finally get a chance to see some of this wonderful world!"

"Us, too!" I said. Then, nudging Frankie, I added, "And maybe we'll get to leave Detective Fix behind."

We all clambered down the plank and onto the dock.

"Ah, Bombay," said Sir Francis Cromarty, wiping his forehead. "One of the gems of all of India. Today in Bombay there is a festival of one of the religious groups known as the Parsees. They have wonderful customs, very colorful, very musical."

"Indeed?" said Fogg, glancing coolly at his watch. "The train for Calcutta leaves in just over half an hour. Passepartout, you have your errands. Everyone, if you please, we shall meet at the train station in exactly thirty-three minutes beginning . . . now! Do not fail!"

"I shall not!" said Passepartout.

"Us not, either!" I said.

With that, Fogg and Sir Francis strode off toward the train station to get tickets. That left Frankie and me alone with Passepartout at the foot of a huge city.

"We don't get much time to look around," I said, staring at all the pink and orange and purple buildings.

"That's the whole problem with life," said Frankie.

"There's always too much *stuff* to do. You can't enjoy the best things. Like just wandering around."

"I agree with Frankie," said Passepartout. "Are we to miss Bombay as we have missed Paris and Rome?"

"It does seem harsh," I said. "Besides, what trouble can we get into in just . . . thirty-two minutes?"

The first thing we found out as we wandered into the city was that Sir Francis was right. There really was a religious festival going on. Down one street of pink stone buildings there came a parade of people dancing to the sound of tambourines and drums and strange, whining musical instruments.

"Awesome!" said Frankie.

"Let's follow the parade," said Passepartout.

"Maybe there's food at the end of it!" I added.

The parade wound through narrow streets and up a hill to a giant temple with a big pointy dome on top.

"A lost temple!" I said. "How cool can you get?"

Frankie gave me a look. "It's not lost if everybody knows about it."

Passepartout was doing his own little dance and heading toward the big building.

"We should go after Passepartout," I said.

Frankie chewed her lip. "I don't know. . . ."

"It looks like fun. I'm going!" I rushed after him.

Frankie grumbled, but soon caught up with us. Together, we slid through one of the pointed archways and into the temple. The high dome was deco-rated inside with tiny colored tiles, some of which were gold. Light filtered down through openings around the top, shedding streams of colored light across the floor.

It was cool and hushed inside the huge room.

"It's beautiful!" Passepartout whispered.

"I've never seen anything so amazing," I said, try-ing to look at everything at once. "It's so quiet and peaceful in here. The place is full of people, but you can't even hear anyone walking around."

"That's because they've taken their shoes off," said Frankie. "Look, nobody has shoes on but us."

It was the "but us" part that should have warned me.

Within a nanosecond, there was a gang of wor-shipers running toward us. "Stop them!" they shrieked.

Frankie and I took off running. Passepartout wasn't so lucky. Someone stopped him and pulled off his shoes.

"My wonderful French shoes!" he cried. He managed to twist out of their grasp and, slipping and sliding in his socks, tore across the floor to the exit. Meanwhile, Frankie and I had zipped out and clam-bered up to a sort of porch above the temple door.

"But I didn't do anything!" cried Passepartout,

facing an even larger crowd rushing at him from the street.

"It looks like we offended them by wearing shoes in the temple!" Frankie called down to Passepartout. "Now jump up to us!"

Just as the crowd closed in, Passepartout jumped up and grabbed our outstretched hands. Amid the screaming of the throng, the three of us leaped from one colorful roof to another and finally down into the street.

We didn't stop until we boarded the train.

Chug! Ssss! The engine puffed a huge cloud of steam and began to roll away. An instant later, the angry worshipers skittered into the station, screaming at the top of their lungs, and waving Passepartout's shoes in the air.

At the same moment, too, Detective Fix raced onto the platform. But the train was already too far along to catch. You would think the guy would be mad.

Instead, he smiled at the crowd of angry temple worshipers and then, from far away, at us.

"I don't like the way he's looking at us," I said.

"Then you won't like this look, either," said Frankie.

I turned around to see Mr. Fogg glaring down at us.

Chapter 8

"I believe I asked you not to get into trouble," said Mr. Fogg as the train chugged on.

"I've heard about your little escapade," he said when we wormed our way to our compartment. "We must hold all local customs in great respect."

"Quite right," said Sir Francis, who occupied the seat next to Fogg. "The government is very severe about this sort of thing. Quite against the law to wear shoes in an Indian temple. The worshipers get angry, you know."

"We found out," I said. "It won't happen again."

"I am especially sorry," said Passepartout, pulling on a pair of slippers and hanging his head the way I do when Mr. Wexler catches me daydreaming.

"Very well," said Fogg. And that was the end of it. He began scribbling in his notebook, and everyone else was fairly quiet for the next few hours. The train chugged swiftly into the evening.

"Passepartout," I said, "what time do you have?"

He pulled out his watch. "Seven in the evening."

Sir Francis laughed. "You are over four hours slow!"

Passepartout smiled. "Perhaps that is because I did not change it from London time."

"What difference does that make?" I asked.

Sir Francis smiled. "It is seven in the evening in London, four hours earlier than it is here, because you have been traveling eastward."

Instantly, my head began to hurt. I guess it showed.

The military man leaned forward. "You see, the earth is divided into three hundred and sixty degrees all the way around. Since your journey is taking you to the east, you gain four minutes with each degree you pass through. And I should guess that you have passed through some seventy degrees so far. That accounts for the four-hour time difference and why it is earlier in London than it is here in India. Do you understand now?"

"Sort of," said Frankie.

"Sort of me too," I said. "Okay, not really."

"At any rate," said Passepartout, stuffing the watch back in his pocket, "I will not change my watch to suit the place. It shall remain on London time!"

"Quite right," said Mr. Fogg. "Now, if you will excuse me . . ."

Instantly the conversation stopped, and Fogg huddled over his notebook again and scribbled in it, pausing only to look at his own watch and to mumble softly.

It was boring watching him, so Passepartout, Frankie, and I decided to go out to the back platform to get cool.

"What a master!" said Passepartout. "He refuses to look out the window. We are traveling across India, and he sees none of it! I am sorry about losing my shoes, but at least we saw some of Bombay. Him! He only looks into his little tiny book and scribbles with the numbers. An hour behind. A day ahead. Aye-yi-yi!"

"He is an odd sort of guy," said Frankie. "I wonder if he cares about stuff the way normal people do."

The train shot away into the darkness of the Indian night. Looking around, we could see the huge, wide night sky dusted with stars, and the strange shapes of temples and large, shaggy trees filling the background.

Sir Francis came out onto the platform, just as the

train whizzed past a group of elephants tramping slowly beside a river that ran parallel to the tracks.

"We will be entering the dark section of the country soon," said Sir Francis. "But we are perfectly safe as long as we remain on the train."

"I don't like the sound of that," I said, gazing into the scenery blurring along beside us. "What's out there?"

"Tigers and snakes and other creatures of the wild are the real rulers in these jungles," Sir Francis said. "Then, of course, there is the village of Kalenger. . . ." He suddenly went quiet.

I turned to Frankie. Her eyes were wide. She was paler than usual. She nudged me. "You ask."

"No, you."

"I asked you first."

I took a deep breath. "Um, excuse me, Sir Francis . . . what about the village of Kalenger?"

Sir Francis's voice went almost to a whisper. "The villagers there are devoted to the Indian goddess . . . Kali."

"Collie?" I said. "Lassie was a collie. She was nice."

"Not collie," said Frankie. "Kali. Go on, Sir Francis."

The old military guy sucked in a long breath, looked both ways into the night, then stared right into our eyes. "The followers of Kali call her the god-dess of *death*!"

Frankie and I nearly jumped out of our skin.

"You do well to be afraid," said Sir Francis. "The followers sacrifice victims to Kali, right here in these jungles just a few feet away from us. They don't like strangers, that's for sure."

I raised my hand. "When you say *strangers*, um, do you, sort of, you know, mean, like—"

"Us," he said.

Frankie gulped. "Us? As in . . . us?"

"Us!" Sir Francis said creepily. Then he laughed. "But we have nothing to fear! This railway doesn't stop in the village of Kalenger! We won't be anywhere near where the villagers do their dark deeds! This train shall rumble right through until the morning light—"

Errrrrch! The train screeched to a stop.

"Passengers, into the jungle now!" the conductor yelled. "The railway ends here!"

Chapter 9

In a flash, Phileas Fogg was out of his compartment and hopping off the train next to us. At the head of the train were some tents pitched in a small clearing, a bunch of workmen, and a bunch of no more tracks.

"What is the meaning of this?" asked Mr. Fogg, to someone who looked like he was in charge. "Why are we stopped here?"

"The railway is not finished!" was the answer.

Even in the dark night, I could tell that Passepartout was getting all red-faced. "Impossible! Do you know that my master must cross India in three days! How are we to do this now?"

I went up to the train guy myself. "Look, Frankie

and I are stuck here in your world unless we make it completely around the world in eighty days!"

The man shrugged. "Good luck with that. The rail line begins again in Allahabad, fifty miles from here. Good-bye."

"But . . . but . . ." Passepartout stammered.

"No matter," said Mr. Fogg. "We shall find another way to Allahabad. There must be some way to—"

Rrrooo! A loud trumpeting sound interrupted him.

Mr. Fogg turned. "I say there must be some way—"

Rrrooo!

We turned and saw an elephant ride by. On his back was a small man dressed in a yellow robe and turban.

In a flash, Mr. Fogg unclasped his carpetbag and took out a wad of bills. "Excuse me, sir, I should like to purchase your elephant. Is two thousand pounds enough?"

Rrrooo! This time it was the owner who was making the happy sound. He slid down from the elephant's back, snatched up the money, and gave Mr. Fogg the reins to his giant gray friend.

Passepartout scoured the village and found a young man named Jahib, an elephant driver who said he could take us to where the train tracks started up again.

"But it is best not to travel at night," Jahib said. "We would do better to start in the morning—"

"Impossible," said Fogg. "We must leave tonight."

Jahib shrugged, climbed up the elephant's trunk to his head, and sat there. "As you wish. Let's go!"

In a matter of moments, we were all on board the huge elephant, whose name we found out was Kiouni—which Jahib pronounced Kee-OOO-nee. We were crammed into something called a howdah, which is a big open box on the elephant's back, sort of like a saddle.

Jahib patted Kiouni's head and—*rrrooo!*— Frankie, Sir Francis, Passepartout, Mr. Fogg, and I, with Jahib at the wheel, were on our way.

The jungle was thick, and Kiouni was forced to take a twisted path through it, tramping down the overgrowth with each thundering step.

"If we reach Allahabad tomorrow evening," said Mr. Fogg, "we shall be less than a day overdue. Not bad."

"The badness hasn't come yet," said Jahib, suddenly raising his hand sharply, which I took to mean for us to keep quiet. The elephant stopped abruptly.

Everyone went quiet and listened.

Then we heard it. A kind of confused murmuring coming through the thick branches. The noise grew louder, and the murmuring more distinct. It seemed like human voices accompanied by instruments.

"Wait here," said Jahib. He jumped to the ground and crept stealthily through the jungle trees. A moment later, he was back. "A procession is coming this way," he whispered.

"A parade, like in Bombay?" I asked. "That was sort of fun. Well, until Passepartout lost his shoes . . ."

Jahib shook his head. "This is not quite the same thing. They must not see us. Hide!"

We did hide. Jahib led the elephant into a thicket of branches and vines. We all held our breath.

The voices and strange instruments drew nearer.

The head of the procession soon appeared. First came what looked like priests, dressed in long robes. Then the singers who chanted and droned a very scary song. Behind them was a kind of cart with large wheels, with spokes carved like serpents. On the cart stood a scary statue with four arms, a red body, and crazy hair.

"Kali!" Sir Francis muttered. "Goddess of death."

Frankie turned to him. "You mean—"

"The villagers of Kalenger!" Sir Francis whispered.

I glanced at Frankie. Her face was pale. "You scared?"

She nodded. "Beyond scared."

"Yeah, me three."

Following the cart was a group of muscle men armed with swords. They were leading a woman dressed in jewels and gems, bracelets, earrings, and rings.

"She's sort of very pretty," Frankie whispered.

The lady was wriggling and twisting in the grasp of the big guys around her. It didn't look good for her.

"She's sort of trying to get away, too," I said.

At the end of the parade was another cart. Lying on it was an old man, all dressed in white and wearing a turban of gold silk dotted with pearls. He was not moving very much. Okay, at all. If you know what I mean.

"Neat outfit," I said. "Too bad the guy can't enjoy it."

"Hush!" said Mr. Fogg, not taking his eyes off the procession as it slowly wound under the trees and disappeared in the depths of the jungle. Soon it was gone.

"That," said Sir Francis, "was a suttee. A human sacrifice. The villagers will take that poor woman's dead husband and set his body afire. And she will join him."

"When will they do this terrible deed?" said Mr. Fogg.

"Tomorrow at dawn," said Jahib. "At the temple of Pillaji, where all their ceremonies take place."

Phileas Fogg wrinkled his brow. "I see," he said. He pulled out his notebook and scribbled in it for a while, looking away for a second as if he were calculating some kind of math problem. Then he put the notebook away with a simple nod of his head.

"Suppose we save this woman?" he said.

Sir Francis nearly jumped out of his boots. "Save the woman, Fogg?"

Mr. Fogg nodded slightly. "I have some twelve hours to spare before I am officially late. I can devote those hours to this task."

Passepartout nearly kissed his master. "My master! You are a man with a heart after all!"

"Sometimes," Fogg replied. "When I have the time."

Chapter 10

Creeping through the jungle quietly and carefully, we reached the temple at midnight. Jahib, wanting to rescue the woman as much as we did, led the way. Fogg was second, and Sir Francis third.

Passepartout, Frankie, and I brought up the rear.

"I believe my master has a heart, after all," Passepartout whispered to us, his eyes twinkling.

"Let's hope it doesn't come spilling out all over the place," I said. "These guys don't look like the friendliest people in the world."

"They are quite ruthless," Sir Francis agreed.

The procession wound its way to this enormous temple of black stone towers and arches, with torches hanging from the walls. Before the temple was a sort of open area like an oversize patio, except that in the center was a very tall bed piled high with flowers and sticks.

"The flowers make it look all fluffy and nice," I said. "Makes me think of going to sleep."

"Eternal sleep," said Sir Francis. "That bed is where the sacrifice will take place."

I gulped. "Suddenly, I'm not tired anymore."

While we waited for the procession to finish, Jahib told us about the woman being drawn into the square by the guys with swords.

"Her name is Aouda," he said, pronouncing her name Ahh-OOO-da. "She was educated in London as a child and speaks perfect English. When she came back to India, she was married against her wishes to the old rajah, who was a sort of nobleman. Marrying him made her a princess. But now, because the rajah has died, by the harsh rules of the villagers the princess must die also."

I shivered. The thing was so wrong and creepy, I knew we were right to stop it. But the place was crawling with swords and spears and daggers and pointy things of all shapes and sizes carried by guys of mostly one shape and size—huge!

We got as close as we could but stopped a couple of hundred feet away from the square. The procession ended at the wooden stage when they brought the dead rajah up and laid him on top of the flowery bed.

Aouda was taken into the temple where the music and singing and dancing kept going, getting louder by the minute.

"This is all part of the suttee," said Sir Francis. "It's rather like a party at first, then the sacrifice."

Frankie shivered. "So what do we do now?"

"We need to get closer," said Mr. Fogg. "But surely we will be spotted as outsiders. If we had a distraction, we might slip into the temple and rescue the princess."

It sounded so cool to be rescuing a princess. I looked over at Frankie. She was looking at me. We were both thinking the same thing.

"Disguises!" she said.

"My thought, exactly," I said. "Listen up, people. While Frankie and I distract the crowd, you see if you can free the princess. We'll all meet back at the elephant and scoot out of here, okay?"

"Let us all do our parts," said Fogg. Everyone nodded. At the count of three, we all flew into action.

Frankie and I slid back through the trees to the elephant and whipped a few pieces of cloth out of the howdah saddle box. I wrapped one around my head like a turban and another around me like a robe. Frankie did the same. We were completely ready.

By the time we made it back to the temple, I

couldn't see Passepartout, but I spotted Fogg and Sir Francis creeping around the edge of the crowd. Jahib was ready to charge in at a moment's notice with Kiouni.

Just then, a bunch of armed guards brought the princess out of the temple. They tied her down next to the old dead rajah on the flowery bed.

"Ready?" said Frankie.

I gulped. "As ready as I'll ever be. Let's go!"

Frankie and I jumped into the throng of singing, dancing, shouting people.

"Excuse me!" I shouted at the top of my lungs.

The whole ceremony stopped. Everyone went quiet. They stopped all the chasing and the waving around of swords and gawked at Frankie and me strolling around the temple grounds as if it were a garden.

"Do not harm that princess!" I shouted.

In the light of the torches the villagers carried, their eyes glowed like fiery flame. I quivered but went on.

"We are traveling on a world tour with Phileas Fogg, a gentleman of London!" I said. "We have only eighty days, which means we need to be on our way soon. So, we'll just be rescuing that princess—"

"Who, by the way, you shouldn't be burning," added Frankie, "because it's just very wrong!"

The villagers were all so shocked that, for a second, it seemed as if they might actually let us do what we wanted.

Then the second was over.

"You are not in London now!" one villager shouted. "And you are trespassing on a private sacrifice!"

"Hmm," I said. "You make a good point."

"And my point," growled another of the villagers with a humongous sword, "is aimed right at you!"

"Difficult to argue with," said Frankie.

But just when the whole army seemed ready to charge us with swords, there came a terrible, ear-piercing scream from the flowery bed.

Everyone turned to see the old rajah—the old *dead* rajah—suddenly bounce up lightly from the stick pile, yell out, "Aye-yi-yi!" and hit the ground, running.

And running next to him was—Princess Aouda!

"Whoa, the guy moves fast for an old dead rajah," I said.

He sure did. An instant later, he dashed by us, saying in a familiar French accent, "Let us be going— now!"

"It's not an old dead rajah!" said Frankie. "It's— Passepartout!"

"I had a plan of my own!" said the Frenchman. "I hope my master does not object?"

60

"Not at all," said Phileas Fogg. "But I suggest we—"

"Get out of here!" I cried.

But we wouldn't have gotten out if not for Jahib.

Rrrooo! Roaring at the top of his lungs, Kiouni thundered at full speed through the crowd of angry, sword-thrashing villagers and right up to us.

In an instant, Passepartout, the princess, Sir Francis, Mr. Fogg, Frankie, and I leaped on board and galloped away into the midnight jungle!

Chapter 11

It was only after about an hour of crashing through trees and leaves, everyone bouncing around the howdah, that Passepartout finally stopped chattering.

"It was a little plan of my own!" said the Frenchman, grinning from ear to ear. "I saw the crazy crowd and thought, they will not see me worming my way through them. They will not see me hide the old rajah under the flowers and take his place. And they did not!"

"Well done!" said Sir Francis shaking the servant's hand vigorously. "Well done, I say!"

"But all the credit goes to my master," said Passepartout, calming down. "If not for him, we would have passed by without even trying to save the princess!"

Mr. Fogg nodded quietly. "Well, I had the time."

"I wish to thank you," said the princess, gazing at Fogg with these amazingly deep eyes. "But how can I ever repay you for such a deed as saving my life?"

"Not necessary, I assure you," Fogg replied. "Now, Jahib, let's make haste to Allahabad. By my calculations, the train will be leaving there for Calcutta in exactly three hours. I would very much like to be on it."

As Jahib drove the lumbering Kiouni through the jungle at an even swifter pace, Frankie nudged me.

"He doesn't even notice," she said.

"Who doesn't notice what?" I asked.

"Fogg doesn't even see that Aouda likes him."

"He doesn't?" I said. "I mean, she does?"

"Talk about being in a fog!" Frankie snapped. "It was his decision to rescue her from ultimate death, right? Well, now she's safe and free and grateful and . . . you fill in the blanks. I mean, look at her."

Now, I'm not into all that romantic goop they shovel at you on television. I mean, ick. And I'm not sure if Fogg noticed Aouda or not. But I have to say, she did seem to be looking at Mr. Fogg a lot. And she was fairly good-looking. Plus, she was a princess.

Soon, we came out of the jungle to the small city of Allahabad, where the railway picked up again. A loud spurt of steam nearby told us that the train was there and ready to leave.

"Fine work, Jahib," said Mr. Fogg, sliding down from Kiouni, the elephant. "You have kept us on time after all. As a reward, I should like you to keep Kiouni, as a present."

"Mr. Fogg!" said Jahib. "Such a gift!"

Fogg bowed. "It is enough that you make Kiouni happy. He has been a great help in our efforts."

We had to say good-bye to Kiouni, but it was okay because Jahib was so happy and we knew he would take good care of her. And we would always remember the cool jungle rescue adventure we had.

"That's the thing about trips," said Frankie, looking misty eyed. "You go to new places and meet great people, but then you have to say good-bye to them, too."

I understood. "It's too bad you can't just hold on to everything. Like the jungle rescue. It was fun, but now it's over."

"Perhaps there is more to come," said Passepartout. "If only we make our connection!"

And with a *fwit-fwit-fwit!* we were on the train, rattling and chugging its way out of Allahabad toward the city of Calcutta.

With all six of us settled into our compartment, we entered jungle after jungle where we heard the roaring of tigers and howling of wolves. I was sure glad to be in a train that wasn't going to run out of track anytime soon.

Since we had time, Frankie settled back with her nose stuck in the book. After about ten minutes she grinned.

"What's going on?" I asked her.

"Watch this." Then turning to Sir Francis, she asked, "What happens to Aouda, now that we've rescued her?"

"Surely, she will be hunted down," said Sir Francis.

Fogg glanced at a page in his notebook, then looked up. "Then she shall accompany us to Hong Kong."

"My cousin is a merchant there!" Aouda said.

"Good," said Fogg. "Everything will be mathematically arranged in Hong Kong."

Her eyes filled with tears and we could see that she was really grateful for everything and grateful especially to Mr. Fogg for stopping his journey to rescue her.

"But let us not lose sight of the main point," said Fogg. "We are twenty-three days into our journey. The steamer leaves Calcutta for Hong Kong today, October twenty-fifth, at noon. We must be on it."

The train kept chugging along through the fields and farms. Finally, at around eleven in the morning, the scenery began to thin out, and a great city lay ahead.

"Calcutta, with one hour to spare," said Passepartout.

The train pulled into the station and slowed to a stop.

"It's time for me to say good-bye," said Sir Francis. "Mr. Fogg, Passepartout, Aouda, Frankie, Devin, I doubt whether leading my battalion will be as exciting as our adventures together. Well, then, good-bye!"

He saluted, and we saluted him back.

"Now to the steamer," said Mr. Fogg. "We have fifty-one minutes to make the connection. Steamer, ho!"

But it wasn't going to be so easy to ho any steamer. Because as soon as we stepped off the train and onto the station platform, a voice yelled out, "Stop—all of you!"

We whirled around, and there was a policeman standing there with several officers behind him. "Excuse me, are you Phileas Fogg?"

"I am," said Fogg.

"Then, in the name of the British Government," the policeman said, "I ask you to follow me at once."

Without a word, we followed the policemen to a big courthouse in the center of Calcutta. Inside, we were led to a small courtroom. We were told to sit on a bench opposite a high desk where the judge sat. He glared down at us. "Bring in the witnesses!" he boomed.

A door swung open, and three guys wearing long robes came in. One of them spoke. "We charge Mr. Fogg's servant and his companions of trespassing on a holy temple!"

I jumped up. "Oh, yeah? Well, we charge them with trying to kill this princess here!"

The judge banged that hammer of his on his desk. "What are you talking about? Bring in the evidence!"

A policeman entered and slapped two things down hard on the courtroom desk in front of Passepartout.

"My wonderful French shoes!" he squealed. "How did they get here?"

But as I watched Passepartout jump up and down about his shoes, it suddenly struck me exactly how they had gotten there, all the way across India from Bombay to Calcutta. I whirled around and saw the reason. He was was trying to hide in the shadows, but I saw him.

"Fix!"

I grabbed the book. Flipping back a few pages, I reread the part where Fix twisted his weird little mustache tips at the Bombay train station.

"His devious little brain was planning this all along," I whispered to Frankie. "To get us thrown in jail and delay Mr. Fogg's trip!"

"Yeah?" Frankie snarled. "Well, it's working."

"Your trial shall be next week," boomed the judge. "And Mr. Fogg shall also be held accountable for the acts of his servant."

Passepartout squealed again, this time in outrage. "But we shall miss our steamer! And lose our wager!"

"Excuse me," said Mr. Fogg. "Judge, may we be set free by posting a certain amount of money as bail?"

The judge breathed out heavily. "I suppose I must grant you that right. I hereby set bail at two thousand pounds. Once you pay, you will be free until the trial."

Mr. Fogg calmly plunked down his giant carpet-bag, withdrew a wad of cash, and set it on the judge's desk. "Two thousand pounds, sir."

"You may go, for now," said the judge.

Twenty minutes later, Fogg led us to the Calcutta harbor where the steamship *Rangoon* was moored.

"Mr. Fogg, you shall lose your money," Aouda said.

"The money is not important," said Fogg. "As long as we do not lose a moment. And on we go!"

As we tramped up the plank and onto the ship, I turned to Frankie. "I'm sure glad to leave Detective Fix grumbling in the background."

"Something tells me he won't give up so easily," she said.

Unfortunately, Frankie was right.

Chapter 12

The steamship *Rangoon* sailed past a bunch of cool islands as it steamed south from Calcutta. Vast forests of palm trees, green bamboo trees, and wild ferns sprouted out of the islands, while hot breezes swept over the deck and the ship rolled over the waves.

Still, Detective Fix was all we could think about.

"As unbelievable as it sounds, Devin, I know he's on board," said Frankie, as we patrolled the deck. "I haven't seen him, but I feel him lurking."

"I do, too," I said. "I say, we go on the prowl right now."

Well, we didn't have to prowl more than a minute before we saw a sneaky guy darting up the stairs from a lower deck. It was Detective Fix, all right, in his regular suit, pointy mustaches, and all.

I snorted. "This guy never quits. Let's follow him!"

Fix crept along behind Fogg and Aouda, muttering stuff to himself. We skulked along behind the skulker.

"I lost him in Suez, I lost him in Bombay," he was muttering to himself. "I lost him in Calcutta. If I don't delay him for sure in Hong Kong, I will have lost him for good!"

I turned to Frankie. "He's just so evil!"

"You get no argument from me," said Frankie.

"And who is this woman?" Fix wondered aloud.

Even before Fix wandered off into the shadows again, we had something new to worry about.

A ferocious storm whipped up from nowhere and began tossing the ship roughly from side to side.

Passepartout came stumbling out of his cabin, shaking his fist at the sky and saying things in French that didn't sound all that good.

Frankie and I were a little panicked, too, but there was not much we could do about it. We could reread all we wanted, but the book's pages got all blurry when we started to read beyond where the story was.

Through it all, Mr. Fogg stood at the railing and gazed at the storm as if it were a still life. Nothing seemed to bother him. While Passepartout almost

70

had a stroke with his moaning and groaning about possibly missing our next ship, the *Carnatic*, our fearless leader was so calm you would have thought the storm was part of his plans.

"He's very strange," I said, trying to keep from getting pitched overboard. "I mean, I like him, but I wonder if he's really human."

"Yeah. It's like everything with him is mathematical and exact. Sometimes, I just want to run up behind him and yell 'Blaga-blaga!,' just to see what he'd do."

"He'd probably just say— 'Blaga-blaga, *indeed*!'"

Splash! A big wave washed over the deck.

"Let's get inside," I said. "The book's getting wet. Not to mention me!"

The storm blasted and howled for two days before it finally let up. Even though we lost a day, when we got to Hong Kong—on November 7, thirty-six days after leaving London—the steamship *Carnatic*, bound for Japan, was still waiting in the harbor.

"We set sail at five o'clock in the morning," said the captain of the *Carnatic*. "Bright and early."

"Arrgh!" Fix muttered to himself.

"What luck!" said Passepartout.

"There is no such thing as luck," Mr. Fogg noted, scribbling in his book. "Now, Princess Aouda, as we are in Hong Kong, we must find your cousin."

The look she gave him then would have melted most people into a puddle, but Fogg appeared not to notice.

We all got into a carriage and rode through the streets of Hong Kong. It was a busy place, with hundreds of buildings crowded into a small half-circle of mountains that slanted right down into the sea. There were English soldiers everywhere, and a lot of the people were dressed like the people back in London.

Fogg found where Aouda's cousin lived, but it turned out that he had moved to Holland two years earlier.

A look of distress crossed Aouda's face. In her sweet, soft voice, she said, "What should I do, Mr. Fogg?"

Without a pause, Fogg said, "Princess, I should be honored if you would come with us the rest of the way."

She practically leaped for joy. "Oh, Mr. Fogg—"

"Once in London," Fogg continued, "we can make arrangements for your journey to Holland."

Aouda unleaped for joy. "Oh. Yes. Thank you, of course." I don't think she wanted to hear that last part.

"Passepartout," said Fogg. "Go to the *Carnatic*, and purchase five tickets instead of four."

Of course, Passepartout was delighted. He made it no secret that he liked Aouda a lot. He skipped all the way to the ship, and we skipped all the way with him.

And it was a good thing we did, because when we arrived at the *Carnatic* to get tickets, we found that the captain had changed the time for sailing.

"We leave tonight," he said. "At midnight."

"We must tell my master at once!" said Passepartout.

Now, who should appear just then, but Mr. Fix, the sneaky, snaky guy himself, popping out of the shadows with the ends of his mustache twisted up tight.

"Have you heard?" asked Fix when he reached us.

"That you're bad?" said Frankie. "Loud and clear."

He gave us a look. "That our ship will leave tonight."

"And," said Passepartout, "I must tell Mr. Fogg—"

"Wait!" Fix said sharply. Then he grabbed Passepartout by the arm and tried to hold him. "I have something to tell you about your master—"

"Oh, no you don't!" I said. I tried to free Passepartout, but Fix leaped at me and grabbed my hand. I swung around and wriggled free of his grasp. The problem was that I staggered back into Frankie, knocking the book from her hand. It tumbled to the

73

ground, bounced across the dock, and landed right at the feet of Detective Fix. He picked it up.

"Don't read that!" I said.

"Why?" he snarled. "Is it Mr. Fogg's notebook? Does it describe his crime?"

"Crime?" said Passepartout. "What are you talking about?"

"I'm talking about Mr. Fogg being a bank robber!" said Fix. "There, I've told you! Yes, Mr. Fogg is a bank robber making his escape around the world! And I am a police detective sent here from London to arrest him!"

He began to flip a page or two of the book.

"Don't do that!" shrieked Frankie. "Don't read it!"

There was a reason Frankie was shrieking. We had learned the extreme hard way that if you flip ahead of where the story actually is, the whole scene rips in half and darkness crashes down on you. Crashes really hard.

"Oh, the book is evidence, is it?" the detective said, flipping page after page. "It says here, the *Carnatic*, setting sail from Hong Kong at midnight on the seventh of November, directed her course at full steam toward Japan . . . wait . . . what is going on—?"

"Oh, no, it's happening!" I screamed. "Frankie, grab the book! Close it before—"

But it was already too late.

Kkkrrpp! There was a horrible ripping sound, and the sky above us turned instantly black. A sudden large V-shaped tear appeared over our heads.

"Meltdown!" I cried, as we all toppled to the dock in a mess of arms and legs and the flipping, flapping pages of the old and crusty classic book.

"Help!" Frankie cried out.

"Help me, too!" I shouted.

"Sacré bleu!" groaned Passepartout.

But nothing helped. We were all tossed like a salad and tumbled over and over until everything went dark around us. The next thing I knew, the dock had vanished and I was falling, falling, falling—*thud!*

I hit the ground hard. When I scrambled to my feet, I was still at the dock, but instead of its being night, it was now the next morning, and I was alone.

Passepartout was gone. Fix was gone. Frankie was gone. The book was gone.

And something else was gone, too.

Chapter 13

Instead of the really big steamship sitting in the water, there was a really big empty space.

The *Carnatic* was gone. Departed. Left. Not there.

"No, no, no, no," I began mumbling to myself. "This is not good. This is bad. This is very, *very* bad."

I was stuck in—where was I?—Hong Kong, which is in China. Which is very far away from Palmdale. And the only way back home was with Frankie and the book. But I was everywhere they weren't.

"What if I never find Frankie again?" I groaned out loud. "What if everybody left me behind? What if I get stuck here in Hong Kong? What if I never get back to my life? I like my life! All that lying around. All that TV to watch. All that homework not to do. All the books

I never want to read! No! No! No! This—can't—be—happening! Oh, please, someone give me a sign—"

"Indeed."

Now, I've made fun of that word before, but I was never so glad to hear it as just then, when my life was teetering on the edge of extinction. I whirled around and there was Phileas Fogg, calmly glancing at the big empty space that should have been a ship.

With him was the beautiful Princess Aouda.

"Oh, dear. Our ship has sailed," she said softly.

"Indeed," Mr. Fogg repeated.

"Aouda! Mr. Fogg! I'm so glad you found me!" I interrupted. "I woke up here all alone and didn't know what I was going to do and my head started to—"

"Where is Passepartout?" asked Fogg.

The guy doesn't go for people yelling and screaming. So I calmed down. I took a big breath. Then I told them everything that had happened. Well, I tried to. Because being dropped into books has all these rules, Fogg and Aouda only understood part of it. Among the parts they didn't get was about Fix being a detective sent to arrest Mr. Fogg for robbery. Even though I tried about a hundred different ways to say that, Aouda and Fogg just weren't supposed to know it yet. It was then that I heard another voice. A not-so-welcome voice.

"Eh, did someone say my name?"

It was Detective Fix himself, strolling down the dock with a suitcase in his hand. I felt like tackling him right there, for messing up the trip, for grabbing the book, and also for losing Frankie and Passepartout.

But the dude was bigger than me. Besides, I didn't want to be skewered by that mustache of his.

Of course, Aouda and Fogg were polite to him.

"Good morning, Mr. Fix," said Aouda.

"Our ship appears to have left," Fogg added.

"Oh, my!" said the annoying detective, twirling the twisty ends of his stinky mustache and pretending to be astonished. "Has it? How terrible! And the next steamer doesn't leave for a week. Too bad, too bad. Ah, well. Nothing to do about it. Shall we find a hotel and wait here for the week? Here, Miss, let me get your bag—"

"No," said Fogg, putting himself between Fix and Aouda's bag. "The leaving of the *Carnatic* is a minor difficulty, I admit. But you forget, Mr. Fix, that this is the harbor of Hong Kong, one of the great ports of Asia. With a little work, we shall find a ship to carry us across the China Sea to Japan. Devin, Aouda, let's find a ship!"

Fogg and Aouda stepped off quickly.

Fix snarled under his breath. "But . . . but . . . arggh!"

"Ha!" I said, storming off with Fogg and Aouda to find a boat bound for Japan. Fix stumbled along after us, of course. It seemed as if he was attached to Mr. Fogg by some kind of invisible rope. Every place Fogg went, Fix went, too. It was annoying, but I couldn't stop him.

It wasn't too long before Mr. Fogg found a chubby little guy named Captain John Bunsby, standing on the deck of a small sailing boat called the *Tankadere*.

After Fogg explained what we needed, Bunsby said, "It can't be done—"

"Oh, too bad!" said Fix delightedly.

"—the way you suggest, Mr. Fogg," the captain went on. "But if we go to Shanghai, China, you can pick up the American steamer there."

"Very good," said Fogg. "From there, we'll stop in Yokohama, then across to San Francisco, losing no time."

"Except for one thing," I said. "What about Frankie?"

"And Passepartout?" said Aouda. "They are lost— and we have no idea where?"

Fogg wrinkled his brow, slipped out his notebook, and scribbled a few things. Satisfied, he closed the notebook. "I shall do whatever I can to find them."

"Oh, Mr. Fogg!" said Aouda, her eyes getting misty again. "Thank you."

"Not at all," he said. "I shall be back in one hour, and then we sail."

In an hour he was back, explaining that he had alerted the Hong Kong police that if either Passepartout and Frankie were found, they should be put on the next boat to Yokohama. He left a wad of money for tickets and other stuff to help them.

It was pretty much all he could do.

I didn't like the idea of just leaving Hong Kong without Frankie, but I had to trust that if she had the book, she would do okay. Besides, Passepartout was a good guy. He wouldn't let anything bad happen to her.

When Captain Bunsby said it was time, we all got on board—even Fix wormed his way on—and set sail for Shanghai. The wind filled the sails of the *Tankadere*, and we swiftly made our way out of the harbor to open sea.

"If we can reach Shanghai in time to catch the American steamer," said Mr. Fogg, gazing at the water ahead, "and if, for some reason, Passepartout and Frankie managed to get on the *Carnatic* before it left Hong Kong, we can meet up with them in Yokohama. It all depends on making good time now, of course—"

No sooner had he said this than the winds began to blow harder, the sky turned dark, and lightning flashed across the sky.

"Storm coming up!" yelled the captain.

"Indeed," said Fogg, scribbling the word *storm* in his notebook. "Unforeseen, but not yet a problem."

Now I tell you, I don't like these storms that just "come up." One minute, I'm standing on deck, looking out at the water; the next minute, waves are crashing against the hull and I'm hanging over the side, losing my lunch. The only good thing about this storm was that the winds pushed the ship faster and farther on its way.

Except that it turned out not to be just a storm.

"It's a tempest!" said Fix, waves splashing over him.

"It's not a tempest!" said a sailor. "It's a typhoon!"

"It's no typhoon!" cried the captain. "It's a hurricane!"

Except that it wasn't a hurricane, either.

It was Frankie.

Chapter 14

I could tell it wasn't just a regular storm, because the lightning that flashed and the thunder that crashed were different from any storm I had ever seen before.

They were exactly like the kind of meltdown that happens when you read ahead in the book.

And Frankie was reading ahead.

Seeing the sky start to rip in half usually freaked me out, but not this time. It meant that even though I'd get tumbled all around and probably all kinds of wet, Frankie was okay somewhere and reading.

I kept searching the skies for what I knew was going to happen, and sure enough, there it was.

A black V-shaped rip opened up in the sky as if we were all on a page being ripped in half.

Kkkkk! The clouds split apart. The ship reeled and rocked from side to side. Aouda stumbled into Mr. Fogg. He got all flustered and she just smiled at him as he steadied her. Fix slammed into one thing after another like a pinball. I had to laugh.

Finally, I was thrown hard to the deck, and just as I was sloshing across it, heading straight for the heavy mainmast, I found myself tumbling over and over in the darkness. The next moment I was in blazing sunshine, sliding down to earth on something bumpy.

It was a roof. The roof of a pagoda.

The roof of a pagoda—in Yokohama, Japan!

"Devin!" yelled a voice.

"Frankie!" I cried out, flipping up off the curved edge of the roof and straight down into a goldfish pond.

Splursh!

Wet to the bone, I clambered out to see two very familiar people rushing up to help me out.

"Devin! We found you!" cried Passepartout.

"Told you I'd get him here!" said Frankie.

"Yahoo! We're back together!" I said. "But how?"

Frankie gave me a big grin. "After Mr. Fix caused the meltdown at the Hong Kong dock, we found ourselves on the *Carnatic* sailing without you."

"Then, at dawn today, November fourteenth,"

83

said Passepartout, "we arrived in Yokohama. We got off to wait."

"But we weren't sure if you guys would get here on time," said Frankie. "So I did some reading."

I laughed. "And *splash! boom!*—here I am, in the next chapter. So, okay. If the *Tankadere* set sail November seventh, and today is November fourteenth, that's seven days. Fogg and Aouda should be here soon. It also explains why I'm so hungry. I could eat a . . . a . . . a lot!"

"Me, too!" said Frankie.

"Let us go hunting for food!" chirped Passepartout.

Our noses led us right to the marketplace in downtown Yokohama. Stall after stall sold fresh fish, fruit, and vegetables. It looked great, but we had a big problem. We had no money, and none of the food was free.

Wandering some more, we found a bunch of rich shops, teahouses, and restaurants. The people wore silk kimonos and wooden sandals that clacked on the cobblestones, but they weren't giving away food, either.

"We'd better chow down soon," I said, "or I can't be responsible for my actions."

Frankie laughed. "When are you ever?"

Just then, Passepartout saw a sign up on the side of a building. It read:

JAPANESE CIRCUS TROUPE

ACTS OF ALL KINDS

LAST APPEARANCE BEFORE SAILING TO AMERICA

COME ONE, COME ALL!

Frankie grabbed my arm. "Devin, are you thinking what I'm thinking?"

"Sure," I said. "But do they make nachos in Japan?"

"No, I'm wondering if they're hiring people."

"Frankie is right!" said Passepartout. "Perhaps the circus will hire us. And pay us money to buy food! For instance, I can juggle. If I had three apples—"

"If you had three apples," I said, "I'd eat them. Let's get in there now before I start nibbling my fingers!"

We crashed into the theater and hunted down the owner. We pleaded with him to let us into his show.

"I am an expert juggler!" said Passepartout.

"And Mr. Wexler says I'm a clown," said Frankie.

I nodded. "It's true. She gets that all the time."

The man looked us over, then stared at me.

"You. Can you sing?"

"People can't believe it when I sing," I said.

"And *you* won't, either," mumbled Frankie.

"Ah, but can you sing standing on your head?"

"Some people say that's my softest part!" I told him.

"Can you sing on your head with a plate spinning on your left foot and a sword balanced on your right?"

I gulped. "A sword?"

"A nine-bladed sword!" said the man.

Frankie pulled the circus owner aside. "As long as someone tells him which is right and left, he can do it!"

The guy made a noise, then nodded his head. "All right. I'll hire you. Be ready in five minutes!"

Before I knew it, I was singing "The Star-Spangled Banner" while spinning a plate and balancing an ugly sword. Frankie, wearing a bright orange wig, ran around me honking a wacky horn, while Passepartout leaped about, juggling three apples.

At the end of the song, a bunch of real acrobats came tumbling onto the stage and the three of us instantly became the bottom row of a giant human pyramid!

The crowd went wild as each new acrobat climbed to the top. And it got heavier and heavier for us.

"I can't do this!" I grunted to Frankie.

"If we collapse, everybody falls!" said Passepartout.

"My—back—hurts—" groaned Frankie.

It was exactly at this moment, with about a

thousand pounds of professional Japanese acrobats on top of us, that the theater door opened and two people entered.

I squinted through the crowd at them.

I couldn't believe my eyes.

I screamed with delight. "Mr. Fogg! Aouda! It's us!"

Moving my lips wasn't so bad.

It was when I nudged Frankie and Passepartout to show them that our friends were here, that I realized I shouldn't have moved my arms.

The moment I did, all those acrobats came crashing down in a huge, squealing heap, spilling out into the first five rows of the audience in a mess that they are probably still talking about.

I say *probably*, because we didn't wait around to see.

In an instant, we were flying out of that theater and racing with Aouda and Fogg through the crowd and up the plank of the steamship *General Grant*, which had just started chugging its way across the Pacific Ocean.

To San Francisco.

California.

The United States of America.

Chapter 15

After all the welcome hugs, we sorted out what had happened after Frankie flipped the pages and zapped me to Yokohama.

Just as the storm pushed the *Tankadere* into Shanghai harbor, Captain Bunsby spotted the steamship *General Grant* making its way toward Yokohama.

They signaled to the steamer, it stopped, and Fogg and Aouda—and unfortunately Fix—got on board.

The *General Grant* then steamed to Yokohama. There, Fogg and Aouda learned that Frankie and Passepartout had been on the *Carnatic* when it stopped there, and went searching for them. When

Aouda spotted the circus, she remembered that Passepartout had been a juggler. She and Fogg went straight into the theater.

"The rest is history," I said.

"And now to the future," said Mr. Fogg as we gathered at the ship's railing and looked ahead. "If we make it across the sea in twenty-two days," he said, "reaching San Francisco by December third, exactly sixty-two days into our tour of the world, we shall have gained two days. Then, if all goes mathematically, we shall reach New York by December eleventh, and London by the twentieth, well in time to accomplish our goal!"

The *General Grant* sure did its part, rolling swiftly over the waves. The ship, by the way, was a large paddle-wheel steamer but was also rigged with three masts and lots of sails. It was definitely the kind of boat to make it over lots and lots of ocean.

One thing I find cool is how authors can make days pass with just a few words on the page. To pass the time, I snuggled in a deck chair and did some reading. Within two or three pages, it was already November 23, our ninth day out from Yokohama. We all happened to be on deck when Mr. Fogg informed us that we were exactly halfway around the world.

"But we've already used up more than half of our eighty days," said Frankie, showing me her watch.

Over forty minutes had ticked by since we had left the library. "Does this mean we're behind schedule?"

The man shook his head slightly. "The traveling will be straighter and swifter from here on. Across the ocean, straight across America, then a steamer to Liverpool, and a train to London. It's quite quick from here on to the joyful conclusion of our journey."

"The joyful conclusion," said Aouda. But when she looked at the coolness of Mr. Fogg, I saw in her amazing eyes something not so joyful at all. She was sad.

Me, too, sort of. I really liked Aouda.

Meanwhile, somebody I didn't like—Detective Fix—hadn't given up his evil quest to arrest Mr. Fogg.

"Yes, yes, I know you don't like me," Fix said, when Passepartout sneered at him one morning. "I still believe Mr. Fogg to be a bank robber, but, for whatever reason, he seems intent on getting back to London. Fine. I will help all I can to ensure he gets to London."

"Why would you help?" asked Frankie.

"I will help him," Fix said, "because it is only when we get to England that we'll know whether he is a gentleman, or a terrible robber. Are we friends, then?"

"Friends?" said Passepartout. "Never! But allies, perhaps. At the least sign that you intend to slow us down, however, I will knock you to the ground."

Fix twisted his mustache. "Fair enough."

Ten days later, on December 3, the *General Grant* entered the bay of San Francisco.

"California," I said.

Frankie and I looked at each other. We grinned.

"You know that Palmdale is only a few hundred miles from here," she said.

"I know. I'm tingling. Should we scoot off and say hello to Mrs. Figglehopper and Mr. Wexler?"

Frankie giggled. "Dude, they're old, but not that old. This is way over a hundred years ago!"

"Maybe we could visit their great-great-grandparents," I suggested.

Frankie looked at me. I looked at Frankie.

We both said the same thing at the same time.

"Nah!"

As Mr. Fogg zigzagged us across San Francisco from the port to the railway station, Frankie and I found that it was full of none of the big skyscrapers we remembered from a trip we took there with our families when we were in kindergarten.

The whole city was all small wooden buildings and low brick and stone ones. Some of the main roads were paved with dirt and huge ruts dug by wagon wheels.

One thing I did remember, though, was the hills.

San Francisco is all steep hills and curvy roads,

and we rode up and down bunches of them to get to the train station where Mr. Fogg shed another couple of pounds from his carpetbag by buying us all tickets.

He even bought Fix a ticket.

"The guy may be as cold as a fish," said Frankie, "but he's polite and generous."

"I hope it doesn't get him into trouble," I said. "I think I'll read some more." I was so hooked by the story, the hours passed quickly. If only Mr. Wexler and Mrs. Figglehopper could see me whiz through a book like that.

The train left in a huff of steam at six o'clock in the evening. It rumbled out of town and across the deserty spaces east of San Francisco. Soon it was nighttime, then morning of the next day. By noon we were already deep into what Mr. Fogg called the Great Basin, which was not a huge sink, but a flat area of land between California and the Rockies.

Everyone jammed up to the windows to get a look, but Frankie and I decided we needed a better view. Scrambling up the short metal ladder to the roof of the car, we ran and jumped from car to car until we were at the front. Soon we entered a flat, wide desert.

"It's awesome out here," said Frankie, sitting cross-legged on the roof. "Where exactly are we?"

I popped open the book again and found the page. "It's called the Great Salt Lake Desert."

"Why do they call it that?" she asked.

"Because it's near the Great Salt Lake," I said.

"I see a city up ahead."

"That's Salt Lake City."

"Sort of ran out of names, didn't they?"

A little while later, as we were passing through what I read was southern Wyoming, the train pulled to a stop before an old bridge. Frankie and I climbed down to take a look. It was a wooden bridge built over a deep chasm in the rocks. A man was standing before the bridge, waving a red flag.

"The bridge is too shaky," he called out to everyone. "Sorry, but it won't bear the weight of the train."

"Leave Detective Fix behind," Frankie whispered.

"And his mustache, too," I added.

"What are we to do here?" Passepartout asked. "Shiver in the freezing cold?"

"I've telegraphed to Omaha, Nebraska, for a train to come to the other side of the chasm," the flag waver said. "You can cross the bridge on foot to meet it."

"When will the train from Omaha come?" Fogg asked.

"Six hours," said the man.

Frankie checked her watch. "No, we can't spare the time. There must be another way."

But no one could think of one. So I cracked that

old classic open and read the next page. "Whoa!" I gasped.

"Do you have an idea?" asked Aouda.

"No, but the train's engineer does. Let's find him!"

The engineer was a little guy in a grease-stained uniform. He sat on a small stool in a small cabin just behind the engine. We told him what the flagman said.

"The bridge isn't safe, it's true," he said. "But, well, it might be possible to get across. If the train got up to its very top speed, it might lessen the train's weight and get us over faster."

I thought about that. "Is it like when you make a running leap, it goes longer than a standing jump?"

The engineer nodded. "A bit like that. I've known it to happen. Once or twice."

Frankie chewed her lip. "Um, not great odds . . ."

But Mr. Fogg turned his head slightly. He almost got excited for an instant. Then he calmly said, "Listen to the boy and the engineer. Their idea seems a good one."

"Whoa, yes!" I said, punching the air. "My idea!"

In an instant, everyone was agreed.

Well, almost everyone. As the train whistled and squealed, then reversed itself, backing up for nearly a mile, Frankie gave me a look. "Devin, I sure hope this works—"

Eeeee! The engine let out a huge loud burst of steam, the engineer pulled the whistle, and the train burst into speed, heading for the wobbly bridge.

Faster and faster we drove. The train rushed along the tracks, gaining more and more speed until we were going nearly a hundred miles an hour. The rails were screaming when we finally reached the bridge.

It seemed as if the train actually leaped from one side to the other. In fact, we were going so fast, no one even saw the bridge. It was over in a flash.

"We did it!" I said, jumping up and down and shaking everyone's hand. "That was my idea, my idea. Did you see that? It was so cool! Did I say it was my idea?"

But Frankie turned me around and made me look out the back of the train. The instant we crossed the bridge, it twisted and wobbled and wiggled and quivered.

Then it crashed in a tangled mess into the river below!

"Nice work, Devin," she said. "Was that your idea?"

I gulped. "Actually, it was the engineer's idea. But who cares. We don't need to go back—"

"We need to go back!" cried Aouda.

I blinked. "Um . . . why?"

"Because we are under attack!" said Passepartout.

"Attack?" I yelped. "Who's attacking us?

Frankie pointed out the window at a band of warriors charging the train.

"Them!" she said.

Chapter 16

The hillsides swarmed with warriors from the Indian tribe known as the Sioux.

"Why are they attacking us?" asked Aouda, taking cover behind her seat.

"I'm not sure," I said, leaning over to get a better look. It was a good thing I did.

Thwang! An arrow shot right through the car, narrowly missing me.

"We just crossed into Indian territory!" shouted the conductor. "They're mad we're trying to steal the land and they don't want us here!"

Thwang! Fwing! Another round of arrows flickered through the car, shattering windows on both sides.

"Someone had better do something," said Fix,

twisting his mustache in fear. "Someone, not me, of course."

"Weasel," I muttered.

Even though we were walking targets, I had to admit that the army of warriors sweeping toward us, driving their horses like the wind, was actually pretty cool.

It was like the movies, only more real.

Everything about these guys looked fast. Their long hair was flying up behind them, and the fringes on their suede pants, and the feathers decorating their bows, made them seem as if they had wings.

"They're trying to stop the train," said Mr. Fogg. "We must help the engineer."

What he was suggesting was dangerous, but he didn't even flinch, just like he didn't when he risked his life to save Aouda. When he bolted through the cars to the engine, Frankie, Passepartout, Aouda, and I followed. Not Fix, of course. He was hiding.

"You shouldn't be here," the engineer shouted over the sound of the engine when we got up front. "If the Sioux stop the train, we'll be captured for sure!"

Urging their horses even faster, some of the warriors were riding parallel to the engine up front. They kept shouting and whooping to one another.

"Let us leave at once," said Mr. Fogg. Then he

calmly led the engineer and the rest of us back into the first car.

Well, almost all of us. At the moment I was about to make my exit, three warriors leaped up from their horses right into the engine room, whooping and hollering and blocking the door so I couldn't leave.

The largest of them turned to me. "Stop the train!" he shouted.

I knew that if the train stopped now, the passengers would be overrun. There would be no helping us.

"Me? Stop the train?" I said. "What am I, a genius?"

"Stop the train!"

I blinked at the dude. "Look at me. Is this the face of someone who knows how to stop trains?"

He pushed right up against me. "This is the face of someone who says . . . STOP—THE—TRAIN!"

I gulped. "Yes, sir." I looked around at all the knobs and levers and cranks and buttons. Any one of them might stop the train. Of course, any one of them might blow up the train, too. I decided to be scientific about it.

"Eeny, meeny, miney—this one."

I pulled back on a long red lever.

WOOO! A huge puff of steam blasted from the funnel and—*ERRRRCH!*—the train bolted ahead even faster.

It was enough to make the warriors lose their balance. I took the chance to dash back into the first car where Frankie was waiting for me.

The Sioux didn't like that and started to chase us.

"Okay, you're angry!" I said as we ran. "We get the point!"

"Not yet you don't!" said one of the warriors. Then he loaded up his bow and shot at us.

At just that moment, Mr. Fogg appeared from nowhere and swung his carpetbag up.

Thwonk! The arrow lodged in the bag. Then Aouda jumped out from behind him, whipped off her slippers, and shot them with lightning speed at the warriors.

As a final move, Passepartout tossed a round of apples, and—*fwing! fwing! fwing!*—the three Sioux warriors raced back to the engine room.

"Thanks for the save, you guys!" I said.

"Think nothing of it," Mr. Fogg replied calmly. "Besides, there is a more immediate problem."

"Staying alive?" asked Frankie.

"In a sense," he said. "The engineer tells me that unless we stop this train at Fort Kearney in . . ." He glanced at his watch. ". . . in two minutes and forty-eight seconds, we will surely be captured. For there isn't another station for miles."

"But getting to the engine is impossible!" said Aouda, pointing through the cars to the bunches of

Sioux leaping onto the train. "They have nearly taken over every car. They will trap us in here."

Meanwhile, the train was thundering over the rails.

Passepartout stepped forward. "I will climb under the cars to the engine and stop the train," he said.

Frankie shook her head. "That's crazy talk, Passepartout. We're way at the back of the train. It's impossible to crawl under the train for that long . . . unless . . ."

"Unless what?" I asked.

She turned to me and grinned. "Unless . . . we go on the roof. We did it before. It's more or less fairly safe."

I looked at her. I blinked. Then I smiled, too. "Come on, Passepartout," I said. "We'll show you the way."

In exactly a few seconds, Frankie and I climbed up to the roof of the car, with Passepartout right behind us. We took a running start and leaped onto the roof of the next car. And the next one, and the next one.

It was an awesome feeling, running up there. I had never felt so excited and nervous, and yet I liked it.

"Frankie," I said, as we made another leap and landed two cars away from the engine. "Here we are, smack in the middle of a life-and-death adventure."

"I know," she said, grinning at me. "Could we be doing anything more cool?"

"I can't believe this is only a book," I said. "Wait a sec, only a book? I don't think I'll ever say *that* again."

"If Mr. Wexler could hear you say that!"

While the train chugged along at top speed, Passepartout came up with his plan. "My friends, here it is. Since the warriors have taken over the engine room, the only way to get the train to stop at Fort Kearney is to unhook the engine from the rest of the cars."

Frankie nodded sharply. "Let's do it."

When we got to the first car, we climbed down the ladder all the way to the bottom, near the wheels. From there, the three of us worked our way along under the car. There were bars and chains and other stuff to hold on to. It was scary.

But, hey, you do what you have to do.

Struggling to the front of the car, we managed to find the iron bar that kept the car attached to the engine. Frankie and Passepartout had to go on one side, and me on the other.

We tugged and pulled and yanked and tugged.

Finally, there was a loud popping sound and the bar twisted up suddenly, knocking all three of us clear of the train. We tumbled to the ground, but Frankie and Passepartout fell on the opposite side of the tracks.

I scrambled to my feet while the engine rumbled

away into the distance at full speed, and our part of the train slowed to a stop right in front of Fort Kearney!

"Frankie!" I cheered. "We did it! Ya-hoo!"

Instantly, a huge bunch of noisy soldiers burst out of the fort, driving the Sioux away into the distant hills.

"Hooray, Frankie!" I shouted again.

But there was no answer.

That's when Aouda rushed over, tears in her eyes.

"Frankie is gone!" she said. "So is Passepartout!"

"Gone?" I said.

Aouda pointed to a plume of dust rising in the distance. "Our friends . . . have been captured!"

Chapter 17

"Frankie . . . gone?"

I still couldn't believe it was possible.

Aouda nodded. "I saw her tumble to the ground and several warriors take her away on a horse. Passepartout tried to help her, but he was taken, too! Frankie and Passepartout were heroes who saved the rest of us!"

Mr. Fogg strode over. "Do not fear. I will find them. But only if we do not lose a moment. Who is with me?"

In a matter of seconds, some thirty soldiers volunteered to go with Fogg.

"I'm coming, too, of course!" I exclaimed.

"I'll stay behind," said Detective Fix, his eyes darting everywhere but not meeting mine or Mr. Fogg's.

"To help the wounded passengers. And to keep Princess Aouda safe, of course."

I didn't trust Fix for a second.

"On second thought, I'll stay, too," I said. There was no way I was going to let Fix out of my sight.

Fogg nodded. "I shall return with our friends."

With a toot on the bugle, the troop left the fort. Not long after they disappeared over a distant hill, the air shrieked with the sound of the train whistle.

"The train!" one of the passengers called out. "They're bringing the engine back!"

Chugging in reverse over the tracks, the lost engine finally came to a stop. Immediately, the engineer and the conductor began hooking up the cars again.

"We have to wait for Mr. Fogg to come back with Frankie and Passepartout," Aouda told them.

"Wait?" said the engineer. "I'm sorry, but the Sioux are still out there. They may attack again. I can't take that risk. Besides, I need to keep to my schedule."

And he did . . . without us. Five minutes later, Aouda, Fix, and I were staring at the train puffing its way across the plains toward Omaha. No sooner was it out of sight than darkness fell, the air turned frigid, and snow began to fall in thick, squashy flakes.

Together we waited on an old, busted covered wagon outside the fort.

"I should have gone with Mr. Fogg," I told Aouda. "I mean, my best friend is out there."

"Mine, too," she said. Then she put her hand on my shoulder. "Mr. Fogg is a brave and wonderful man. If anyone can save Frankie and Passepartout, he can."

I felt a little better. "Yeah. I can't figure him out, but he does come through for people when they need him."

Then I told Aouda about Fogg's giving money to the poor woman in London just before we left.

Her eyes sparkled. "He will return soon."

I heard a noise over my shoulder. It was Fix, growling in the shadows. I stood up. "Did you say something?"

"Fogg won't be back," he said in a low snarl. "He's escaped, is what I think. I never should have let him go."

I narrowed my eyes. "You just wait. Fogg'll be back!"

And he was.

Out of the swirling snow, the troop of soldiers came thundering back to the fort, Mr. Fogg himself in the lead. As they approached, Passepartout and Frankie leaped off their horses and rushed to Aouda and me. We had a big, long, four-way group hug.

"But where is the train?" asked Mr. Fogg.

Aouda told him how it came back, but left again on its way to Omaha. "I'm sorry, Mr. Fogg. The engineer needed to keep to his schedule."

Fogg scratched his chin for a moment. "Then we shall have to find another way."

We all sat on the busted wagon and started thinking.

Not only was the snow coming down in sheets, but the wind was picking up something fierce, too.

"What we really need is a fast way to Omaha," I said, as one blast of wind after another swept across the flat plains and tunneled through the wagon's torn canvas.

"Right," said Frankie, frowning deeply. "But how?"

The canvas filled with wind and flapped and fluttered like a sail, then fell back again. It kept doing that, filling up, then fluttering back, up and back, up and back. Every time it did, the wagon moved a few inches.

Frankie noticed it and made a small gasping sound. "Devin, are you thinking what I'm thinking?"

"Yeah," I said finally. "But why do they call them hamburgers when there's no ham in them?"

"No, look." Frankie pointed to the canvas filling up with wind and the wagon sliding across the snow.

Then I did the small, gasping thing.

"A sailboat!" I cried. "Only instead of a boat, it's a

wagon! Only instead of a wagon, it's a sled! With a sail! A sail that fills with wind! A wind-sail sled!"

In a matter of minutes, Aouda, Passepartout, Fix, Fogg, Frankie, and I took the base of the wagon and put flat beams along each side as runners. Then we mounted a mast and ran the canvas up like a giant sail.

We dragged the thing out where the wind was strong; then we all piled on.

Whooooosh! The moment the wind filled the canvas sail, our crazy sled began to slide across the plain.

"It's a sledge," said Mr. Fogg, nearly cracking a smile. "I rather like it."

"I love it!" cried Passepartout, his eyes all twinkly.

In a matter of minutes, our wind-sail sled was bouncing across the vast plains at more than fifty miles an hour!

Chapter 18

Wump! Boing! Sloosh!

With each strong breeze, our sledge seemed to lift off the ground, spilling high waves of snow up behind it.

"I smell theme-park ride!" I said, clutching the back end of the sledge where Frankie and I were taking turns steering straight toward Omaha.

After sailing full speed through the night, it was around noon the next day that Passepartout leaped up and pointed directly ahead. Before us was a collection of roofs all white with snow.

"Omaha!" cried the Frenchman. "We have arrived! And today is December tenth. If we reach Chicago tomorrow, we shall be in New York by the twelfth!

Perfectly on schedule! Then a steamer. And then England!"

"And then England," said Fogg calmly.

Aouda glanced up at him but said nothing.

Fix did help Passepartout hastily pull down the sail, but we were going so fast it took us about a mile and a half to slow down to a stop! And guess what? We stopped right in front of the Omaha train station.

"Awesome driving, Frankie!" I said, slapping her five.

We rolled off the sledge and into the station just in time—*chug-chug!*—to take the next train to Chicago.

The train whizzed really quickly across Iowa. During the next night it crossed the great Mississippi River. By dawn, we were in Chicago.

They call Chicago the Windy City, but after sailing the plains on a homemade sled, it seemed pretty calm to us. Besides, we didn't see much local weather, anyway, because—*zip-zip-zip!*—we were off one train and onto the next in, like, sixteen-point-seven seconds.

"All aboard the New York train!" shouted a man in a blue uniform. And we were on it.

I kept reading, trading off little bits with Frankie, who was keeping an eye on Fix. During that time, we took a lightning-fast tour of all the states—Indiana, Ohio, Pennsylvania, even New Jersey—between

Chicago and New York. When we finally rolled into the Big Apple, it was nearly midnight the next day.

But before we could even gawk at the Empire State Building, which Frankie told me hadn't been built yet, or meet and greet the Mets, who weren't a team yet, we went rushing off to the pier where all the ships were.

Well, almost all the ships.

The one we needed was missing.

"Where is the transatlantic steamer called the *China*?" Mr. Fogg asked the man at the dock's ticket booth. "It is to leave for Liverpool, England, this morning."

The man in the booth blinked. "I'm sorry, sir. It left forty-five minutes ago!"

The next sound we heard was a loud wailing. It was coming from Passepartout, who was stomping up and down on the sidewalk as if he were trying to go straight back to China itself.

"It is all my fault!" he cried. "If not for me, we would not have been captured by the Sioux. If not for me . . . If not for me . . ."

Mr. Fogg let him speak, then said, "Delays such as those you mention have been accounted for. As this good gentleman has reported to us, we are merely forty-five minutes late. It shall not defeat us."

We all looked out across the dock to the vast

Atlantic Ocean beyond. It was huge. It was wide. We had only nine days to cross it. It seemed completely impossible.

But, as usual, Fogg didn't seem too concerned. "It's all very logical," he said. "We shall simply find a captain speedy enough to take us to Liverpool, England."

"Did somebody mention my name?" said a gruff-looking man from a ship nearby.

Mr. Fogg shook his head. "I merely said we need to go to Liverpool, and we are looking for a captain who is speedy—"

"That's me," growled the man. "My ship is the *Henrietta*, and my name is Captain Andrew Speedy!"

I looked at Frankie.

She looked at me.

"Cut! Time out!" I said. "This seems a little silly. Here we are, in maybe the worst spot we've been in. We need a fast captain to get us across a gigantic ocean, so all of a sudden a guy named Captain Speedy shows up?"

Frankie laughed. "Why not check the book to see if he's really supposed to be in this story."

"Good call." I flipped open the book. I read as far as I could before the pages got blurry. Then I blinked, looked up, then blinked again.

"Dudes, his name really *is* Captain Speedy!"

Chapter 19

"Yahoo!" whooped Frankie, jumping up and down with Passepartout. "Captain Speedy! We found Captain Speedy! Our problems are solved! Holy crow, are we lucky or not—"

"Not," said the captain.

"Please explain that remark," said Mr. Fogg.

The captain made a sort of growly noise in his throat and tugged his long scraggly beard and said, "I'm only going to Bordeaux, France. I can take you to France, and it will cost you plenty, but I don't sail anywhere else. Especially not England!"

"Hmm," said Fogg, gazing off into the distance.

So there we were, with nine minutes left on our watch and no chance of getting to England on time.

The zapper gates were going to be fixed any moment. It looked bad.

"Nevertheless," said Fogg brightly. "We will accept Captain Speedy's offer." He pulled a wad of money from his giant carpetbag, and it was all settled.

We boarded the paddleboat steamer, and within the hour we were on our way. Two hours later, there was a loud banging on the door of Captain Speedy's cabin.

It was Speedy himself banging on the cabin door. From the inside. He was locked in.

"Let me out of here!" he cried. "I demand to be free!"

Frankie and I were guarding the door.

"Sorry, dude," I said. "Captain Fogg says you—"

"Captain *Fogg*!" the guy screamed.

"Yes, Captain Fogg!" I said.

It was so neat. As soon as we were out of New York harbor, Fogg opened his carpetbag again and gave all the guys in Captain Speedy's crew a chunk of money. They happily agreed to sail to Liverpool and lock Speedy in his cabin.

Like a pirate—but the best-dressed and most polite pirate ever—Phileas Fogg had taken over the ship!

More banging came from inside the door, but after

a while the guy's fists gave out, so Frankie and I went up on deck to look for Passepartout. We found him under the chugging smokestacks.

"We are in the North Atlantic Ocean," he said.

I gazed out at the cold black water. "Isn't this where the *Titanic* hits an iceberg and goes down?"

"It looks like the Love Boat's taking a dive, too," said Frankie. "Mr. Fogg is about as cold as an iceberg. Look."

Aouda stood against the railing, shivering. She was as close to Fogg as she could be without actually touching him, but there he was, nose deep in his notebook.

"He's calculating how to hurry back to England the quickest way possible," said Passepartout.

I frowned. "It's like he's counting the days until our incredible, ultimate field trip will be over."

"I know," said Frankie. "It makes me sort of sad."

"Right," I said. "So what happens when the trip is over? Aouda goes to find her cousin somewhere? And Mr. Fogg goes back to playing cards?"

Frankie nodded. "That's the sad part."

"I think perhaps Mr. Fogg is a robot after all," Passepartout said with a sigh.

But I looked at Fogg, remembering when he made the decision to save Aouda. And when he went off to rescue Frankie and Passepartout without a thought.

He wasn't quite a robot then. There was something more there. I was sure of it.

During the first days of our voyage across the ocean, things went smoothly enough. The sails were hoisted high and the *Henrietta* plowed across the waves like a real transatlantic steamer. But on December 19, the seventy-eighth day of our trip, there was a problem.

A big problem.

The wind died to nothing and we ran out of fuel.

All of us were on deck when the first mate ran up to Captain Fogg. "We have no more coal," he said. "We have been going full speed since New York. This has used up our entire fuel supply. Sorry, sir, but we are dead in the water. We cannot move."

Fogg was silent for a moment, then nodded at Frankie and me. "Bring Captain Speedy to me, if you please."

A few moments later, we unleashed the angry captain on deck. He was like his own personal typhoon. He stormed up to Fogg and shouted, "Where are we?"

"Seven hundred and seven miles from Liverpool, England," replied Fogg calmly.

"Pirate!" boomed Captain Speedy.

"I have sent for you, sir," said Fogg, "to buy the *Henrietta*. For I shall be forced to burn her."

"Burn the *Henrietta*! Are you insane?"

"Merely practical," said Fogg. "I must burn all the wood on the ship in order to provide fuel for steam."

"But my ship is worth five thousand pounds!"

"Here is six thousand pounds." Fogg handed him two large wads of money.

This had an instant effect on Speedy. As his quivering hands took the money, a grin covered his face. "For me?"

"For the use of your ship. You may keep what is left of her," said Fogg. "The iron hull and engine are yours. If we do not reach London by eight forty-five, on the evening of December twenty-first, exactly two days from now, I shall lose my entire fortune. So you see—"

Captain Speedy suddenly shouted to the crew. "Do as Captain Fogg commands! Full speed to England!"

Passepartout cheered. Aouda cheered. Even Fix did.

The crew leaped into action. Chairs, walls, masts, rafts, railings, even the deck itself, all were chopped up and shoved into the furnace. Thick black smoke billowed out from the smokestacks, and the ship lurched once more over the waves.

In a matter of hours, there was nothing left of the *Henrietta* but the hull and the spinning paddle wheels. It was no more than a flat hulk speeding over the sea.

But it was enough. When the sun rose at dawn on December 21, Passepartout sighted land. "England?"

"England!" cried Aouda in spite of herself.

We chugged into Liverpool harbor at twenty minutes before noon on December 21, the eightieth day.

We thanked the captain and he thanked us for such a memorable voyage. We stepped out onto the dock.

"England!" said Passepartout. "England!"

"Whoa," I said to Frankie. "I can't believe it. We're nearly done. And we've nearly won!"

"In six hours we shall be London," said Fogg. "That will give us exactly three hours and five minutes to clean up and appear at the Reform Club by eight forty-five this evening. Let us head to the train at once—"

But at that exact moment, Detective Fix stomped over, slapped his hand down on Fogg's shoulder, pulled his badge out, and said, "Phileas Fogg, by order of the Queen of England, I hereby put you under arrest!"

Chapter 20

Detective Fix was a rat.

He wouldn't listen to reason, either from us or from Mr. Fogg who, of course, protested that he was innocent of any crime. Ignoring everything, Fix and his policeman friends took us right off to the Liverpool jail.

Aouda burst into tears when we were led to the cell.

"This pretty much stinks," I groaned. "And I'm not talking just about the odor of this room."

"You'll be taken to London tomorrow," said Fix, with a twist of his mustache. Then he left.

"Tomorrow!" Frankie growled, looking at the watch. It was so close to being the eightieth minute, it was obvious we only had a few hours left. "That'll be too late!"

"We won't get back home," I said.

"I don't even care about getting home," said Frankie. "Fogg is so not guilty, but his life is ruined, anyway. He's spent all his money on this trip, and he'll lose the bet on top of it."

Frankie was right. I hardly cared about the zapper gates anymore. I cared about Fogg and Aouda and Passepartout.

It was way too depressing.

But you wouldn't know it by looking at Fogg himself.

If you came into the cell right then, you would have found him seated calmly on a wooden bench, not even looking angry. He stared at the dirty ceiling for a moment; then he took up his notebook and penciled in a line. It read: *Arrived in Liverpool, Saturday, December 21, 80th day, 11:40 A.M.*

Then he waited, and we all waited with him.

One hour went by. Two hours. Three hours. We had less than seven hours now to make the six-hour journey to London.

Finally, Fogg breathed heavily. "I have tried to meet every obstacle we have encountered. But short of making an escape, there seems little chance now. My money is of no help here, it seems—"

It was at this point that we heard footsteps hurrying down the hall to the cell.

The door swung open and Detective Fix stumbled in, out of breath. "I am s-s-so sorry," he stammered, bowing his head and scraping his feet. "Sir—forgive me—a most unfortunate mistake—the real robber—was arrested—three days ago—you—are free!"

"Yes!" Frankie and I whooped, jumping in the air and nearly hitting the ceiling. Aouda screamed for joy.

"Detective Fix," said Mr. Fogg, narrrowing his eyes.

"Yes, Mr. Fogg . . ."

"I am not fond of you."

"You are not?"

"No, I am not!"

Then, with probably the only emotion he had ever shown in his life, Mr. Fogg clenched his fist and let it fly.

Ka-pow! It landed exactly on the tip of Fix's jaw.

When Detective Fix went down in a heap, we all cheered. When he sat up and rubbed his chin, his mustache was all crooked. "Yes, well, I deserved that, I'm sure."

Before anybody could punch the weasel again, Frankie, Aouda, Passepartout, Fogg, and I were sailing out of the cell and straight to the Liverpool train station.

121

Frankie asked the ticket lady where the superfast express train to London was.

"It left," she replied. "Thirty-five minutes ago."

"Noooooooo!" I screamed. "I'm going to explode!"

"No—more—delays!" cried Frankie.

"I shall order a special train," said Fogg, calmly taking the last few bills from the depths of his carpetbag.

Seconds later, the five of us were on a special train, flashing at top speed out of the station. The engineer really poured on the steam. We roared, we flew, we blurred past what was probably some nice scenery. But we saw none of it. Down to the wire, with only minutes left, the train screeched to a stop in London.

The Reform Club was only minutes away by foot.

But when we looked at the huge clock on the wall of the station, we couldn't believe it.

"I'm going to faint," said Frankie.

"I already did!" I said.

The clock, the big stinking clock on the wall of the station, said it was eight fifty P.M.

Having made a complete tour of the world, we were five minutes late.

Five minutes late!

Fogg had lost the wager.

But that wasn't all.

"Oh, my!" said Aouda. "What is that?"

In a dim, distant corner of the train station was a flickering blue light.

"The gates!" I gasped.

It was true. Mrs. Figglehopper's fizzling, sizzling, sparking, flashing zapper gates were there in the train station. But something was wrong. The lights were getting dimmer by the second.

"Excuse us!" Frankie said.

Together we raced across the giant room.

But by the time we got to the gates, the bright blue light had fizzled out completely.

The gates vanished.

And Frankie and I were stuck in 1872.

Forever.

Chapter 21

"It's not fair!" I said, stamping my feet.

Frankie was quiet for a while, then said, "It can't end like this. It just can't. I mean, what's the point of writing the book if you can't have a happy ending!"

We were five minutes too late.

And everything had changed.

Fogg had no money left. His fortune was gone, all spent in eighty days and five minutes. The rest of it belonged to the members of the Reform Club.

Aouda was in tears. Passepartout, for the first time in his life, was speechless. And Frankie and I were stuck in a world without junk food, CDs, or megahold hair gel.

We must have stared at that clock for an hour. But

it didn't even matter anymore. Time meant nothing now.

"I have lost the wager," said Fogg softly.

It was a short sentence, but it meant everything.

Then, with a sadness in his eyes that I'd never seen before, he said, "Please forgive me—all of you—for dragging you with me on this ill-fated tour of the world."

We all objected, of course, and said that it was the best thing we'd ever done, but Fogg said no more. He just headed quietly back to his house at Number 7, Saville Row, where the story had started.

Of course, we followed him. There was nowhere else to go. Frankie and I had to sort out exactly what we would do. Without the zapper gates, we were lost.

Mr. Fogg told Passepartout to set up rooms for Aouda, Frankie, and me, then left us to be by himself.

"It really is unbelievable," said Frankie when we gathered in Aouda's room.

"Yes," said the princess, her eyes still moist with tears. "After having gone the entire way, overcome a hundred obstacles, faced many dangers, and saved lives—to have this happen! To fail so near his goal by this sudden, unexpected event!"

She couldn't go on. She went to sleep. Soon, so did Passepartout, still in shock at how things had ended up.

"Now what?" I said. "What does the book say?"

"Not much," said Frankie. "We still have about fifteen pages left, but they're so blurry I can't read them. But I don't even want to. When we saw the gates at the train station, it was our last chance to get back before that guy fixed them back at the library."

"Yeah, and now we're fixed. Fixed for good."

"We're as stuck as stuck can be."

I looked around. "So, do we just start living in 1872 now? I mean, what is there to do around now?"

She shrugged. I shrugged. Lots of shrugging going on, but no answers. Mostly, though, after eighty days on the road, Frankie and I were tired.

We found our rooms and went to sleep.

The next morning Fogg called for Passepartout with a message for Aouda. We helped him deliver it.

"Princess," said Passepartout, "Mr. Fogg will remain alone all day, but he wishes to see you in the evening."

"Probably to send you to your cousin in Holland," I grumbled.

"We shall see," said Aouda, becoming suddenly thoughtful. She didn't say much after that.

All through Sunday the house was pretty quiet. Fogg didn't go to the Reform Club as usual. There was no point. Since he had not appeared the night before—Saturday, December 21, at 8:45 P.M.—he had lost the wager. There was no reason for him to see his friends.

At seven thirty that night, Mr. Fogg went to see Aouda. Passepartout, Frankie, and I snuck up to her room and peeked through a crack in the door.

Fogg was seated in a chair near the fireplace. Aouda sat in another chair facing him. Waiting a few minutes before saying anything, Fogg finally spoke.

"Will you pardon me for bringing you to England?"

You could see that Aouda was astonished by the question. "I, Mr. Fogg?" she said. "But I—"

"Please let me finish," he went on. "When I decided to bring you far away from your country, I was rich, and I intended to give you some of my fortune so that you would be free and happy. But now I am ruined."

She looked at him with those laky eyes. "I ask you to forgive me for having followed you and delayed you. Perhaps it is my fault you are ruined."

"I could not let you be hurt," he said. "But that is the past. Now I wish to give you whatever little I have left. It is yours."

"But what will become of you, Mr. Fogg?" she asked. "Surely, your friends—"

"I have no real friends at the Reform Club," he said. "Or family, either."

She took a deep breath. "Solitude is a sad thing

with no one to confide in. They say that two people might bear much more together."

"Indeed," said Fogg. "They do say so."

"Mr. Fogg," said Aouda, rising and taking his hand, "do you wish to have a friend and a family member at the same time? What I mean is, will you have me for your wife?"

There was a strange look in Fogg's eyes that we'd never seen before. He shut them for an instant, then popped them open, and said, "Yes. I do love you, Aouda, and I will be your husband!"

That's when Passepartout crashed through the door and started leaping around the room. But Fogg was too busy gazing into Aouda's incredible eyes to notice.

Yeah, yeah, it was romantic goop, all right. But I sort of liked it. Frankie, of course, thought it was the best thing ever. I could tell just by looking at her wet cheeks.

Passepartout hugged Aouda, then Mr. Fogg, then both of them, then Frankie and me. Lots of hugging going on and lots of bouncing around.

"Passepartout," Fogg said finally, "it is now five minutes past eight P.M. on this quite special Sunday. Please notify the Reverend Samuel Wilson of Marylebone Parish that there is to be a wedding at his church."

"For tomorrow, Monday?" asked Passepartout.

Fogg turned to Aouda. "For tomorrow, Monday."

"Yes, for tomorrow, Monday!" she said.

Passepartout leaped up. "I can't wait!" He zoomed out of the room like a rocket.

"Indeed!" said Fogg, cracking his first smile ever.

After about a minute of Frankie and me standing there, it was clear that Fogg and Aouda didn't really want two kids hanging around.

"Um, hey, Frankie, how about we go find Pass—"

"Good idea!"

In a flash we were out and about in London.

It actually took us a while to find Passepartout, mainly because the London streets were as twisty as Fix's mustache, and partly because Frankie wasn't really helping. She was trying to read the last few pages of the book to see if there were any clues about what might happen to her and me. But, no, the pages were still too blurry to make out any words.

"I guess when the gates died, the story died, too," she said. "I mean, we're making our own story now. Which, let me tell you, is way too weird for me."

Finally, we saw a familiar figure racing along the street toward us.

"Passepartout!" I said. "Slow down. What's wrong?"

But he rushed past us, shrieking, "Must hurry! Tell Mr. Fogg! Must hurry! Oh!"

We hustled to keep up with him as he screeched around the streets. "Did you find Reverend Samuel Wilson of Marylebone Parish?" I asked him.

"Yes!" he huffed. "No time to explain! Must hurry!"

We raced with Passepartout into Mr. Fogg's house.

"What is the matter?" Mr. Fogg asked when we burst into his living room.

"Wedding impossible for tomorrow!" Passepartout blurted out. "No weddings are performed on Sunday!"

"But today is Sunday," said Mr. Fogg.

"No, Saturday!"

"Impossible."

"No," cried Passepartout. "You have made a mistake of one day! We arrived twenty-four hours ahead of time. But now—there are only eleven minutes left!"

Mr. Fogg looked at Passepartout, then Aouda, then Frankie, and me. "Just a moment," he said calmly. "I must understand this."

And with a bare ten minutes left before the *actual* deadline, Mr. Fogg sat at a small table, took out that notebook of his, and began to jot down stuff.

After what seemed like forever, with Passepartout leaping about yelling things like, "Nine minutes! Eight! Only seven minutes!" Mr. Fogg finally looked up at us.

"I see now. The cause of the error is very simple. Without suspecting it, we have gained a complete day on our journey. How, you ask?"

"We didn't ask!" said Frankie. "Let's go!"

Fogg held up his hand. "I will tell you how. As Sir Francis Cromarty reminded us, we were traveling constantly eastward, from London to Suez, India, China, Japan, the United States, then back to London."

"We remember those places!" I said. "Now let's go!"

"Well, in journeying eastward," he went on calmly, "we were always traveling toward the sun. The days were therefore four minutes shorter as we crossed each of the three hundred sixty degrees around the earth. Three hundred sixty multiplied by four minutes equals twenty-four hours. Thus, we gained a day."

Aouda brightened. "So, while you saw the sun go down eighty times, your friends in London only saw it go down seventy-nine times."

"Precisely," said Fogg. "And speaking of my friends, they are no doubt waiting at the Reform Club. Now, as there are one thousand, one hundred fifty-one steps from here to the Reform Club, and five minutes and thirty-two seconds before our time runs out, by my calculations—"

"Stuff the calculations!" I screamed. "Let's get over there—NOW!" I took the book. "Hold on to your hats, everyone! I'm flipping to the next chapter!"

"Devin, don't—" cried Frankie.

But I couldn't take anymore delays. I flipped those blurry pages ahead to the last chapter.

And the whole room exploded in light.

Chapter 22

Kkkkk! The room lit up as if there were fireworks blasting all round us. Then a big black rip appeared up near the ceiling and started toward us.

"Oh, my!" Passepartout yelped loudly. He fell into Mr. Fogg, sending both of them out the door.

Aouda tumbled out of her chair, and Frankie and I spilled into each other on the floor. It was very messy.

Then, suddenly, it was very quiet.

I picked myself up from a very cushy, thick-pile carpet and looked around. It was the Reform Club, all right. Frankie was there. But Fogg was nowhere in sight.

"Don't tell me he didn't make it!" I groaned.

Frankie pulled me up. "Let's check the main room where all the wager guys are. Hurry!"

An orangy light from the gas lamps was flickering all over the old leather chairs and the deep carpet. We crept across the room, trying not to wake up the snoring men.

The wager guys were in the main room, sitting at their usual card table. But they weren't playing cards. They were staring at the huge clock on the wall. The clock said eight forty-one.

"What time did the last train arrive from Liverpool?" one of the men asked.

"Seven twenty-three," replied another. "If Phileas Fogg had been on it, he would have been here by now. We can, therefore, regard the bet as won!"

The others gave a hearty chuckle at that.

The clock ticked away another minute.

"Three minutes left!" Frankie muttered. "Where is he?"

The old guys picked up their cards but didn't play them. They continued staring at the clock, watching the second hand sweep around once more.

And once more again.

It was a moment of deep silence. The whole room was perfectly quiet. At eight forty-four, the men stood and approached the clock, counting the seconds.

"I can't stand it!" I said.

"Shhh!" said Frankie.

"Eight forty-four and thirty seconds," one of the men said. "Forty seconds . . . fifty-two seconds . . . fifty-six . . . fifty-nine . . . and—"

Then, a fraction of a second before the clock chimed the quarter hour, the door swung open and Phileas Fogg stepped into the room.

In his calm voice he said, "Here I am, gentlemen."

Ding! went the clock.

"Ya-hoooooo!" I screamed.

Stunned, the old men quivered and shivered and nearly fainted, but finally they shook Mr. Fogg by the hand, then handed over the money that they'd lost betting against him.

"I have done it in eighty days, gentlemen," said Fogg, now joined by Aouda and Passepartout. "But I couldn't have done it at all without my *real* friends here."

That was, like, the most amazing thing to hear. Frankie and I started to get all misty ourselves.

"This is a good end to the story," Frankie said.

"It is awesome," I said. "But it's not quite the end." I pointed to the next paragraph.

Two days later—which really was Monday—we all piled into the Marylebone Church, and Fogg and Aouda became Mr. and Mrs. Phileas Fogg. Passepartout, grinning so big his smile just about covered his ears, gave the bride away. The newlyweds asked Passepartout to stay on forever as their servant and friend.

Of course, he said yes. After about an hour of jumping up and down.

Then, just as the exit music began playing and we were all leaving the church, we saw it. The blue flickery light of the zapper gates, tucked behind some shrubs by the front walk.

"Frankie, they're back," I said. "We really did do it in time! So the gates still work. We can go back . . . home . . . sort of . . . I guess. . . ."

Frankie must have been thinking the same thing as me. She knew what time it was. But she didn't look all that happy about it.

"I don't want to go home," she said. "Not yet. I mean, we've been completely around the world with these people. We've done everything with them."

I nodded. "Yeah. They're our friends."

We didn't want to go, but we had to. The gates wouldn't buzz and flicker forever. Passepartout grabbed us and embraced us all. We said good-bye to pretty Aouda, who hugged us very tightly, looked at me with those awesome eyes, and gave us kisses.

"We shall miss you," said Mr. Fogg. "I shall miss you. Yes, indeed I shall. . . ."

You could see he was remembering everything that we had done together. All the adventure. All the danger.

Icy cool Mr. Fogg had definitely thawed out.

I couldn't have asked for a better send-off.

Finally, with one last wave, Frankie and I ran straight for the bushes and dived at the glowing zapper gates.

The bright blue light surrounded us completely.

For a split second, we felt all electric and sparkly.

Then everything went dark, as if we were falling into some kind of tunnel. We bounced and tumbled for what seemed like forever, but finally stopped when my head slammed against a big aluminum bookshelf.

After my brain stopped hurting, I realized it was very quiet all around us. As quiet as . . .

"The library," whispered Frankie.

Yep. We were back.

Chapter 23

We were in the library workroom we had left eighty minutes before. And there were the gates, the last little bit of sizzle leaving them.

"Holy crow, were *we* lucky—" I said.

"Shhh!" said Frankie, pulling me down. "I hear someone coming!"

The door swung open and the repair guy entered, his chin covered with traces of powdered sugar.

With him was Mrs. Figglehopper.

"I checked out the gates thoroughly," he said to her. "Backward and forward, top to bottom."

"And?" asked Mrs. Figglehopper.

"They really can't be fixed."

"Oh?"

"Well, they are very old, almost classic," he said. "The newer gates are much more efficient. If you want, I can take these off your hands and use them for parts."

"No!" I wanted to scream, but Frankie poked me.

Mrs. Figglehopper had a strange look on her face, as if she had been half expecting the tech guy to make such an offer.

"No," she said. "These gates have been with me for a long time. I think I'll keep them for a while longer."

It was all I could do to keep myself from jumping around like Passepartout. Frankie sighed with relief.

After the repairman packed up his stuff and left, Mrs. Figglehopper spotted us lurking. "Frankie? Devin?"

We crawled out from behind the bookshelf.

"We were just, um . . ."

"Enjoying your great books!" said Frankie.

Mrs. Figglehopper's eyes did this funny twinkly thing. "Did you enjoy your tour around the world—"

I gasped. "What! So you *do* know about it!"

She tilted her head as if she didn't understand me. "I only meant, did you enjoy your tour around the world of books? That's what every library has, you know. A world of books."

Frankie nodded quickly. "Um, right, we heard. Mr. Wexler told us that, too. And, yeah, it was fun."

The librarian walked us out to the main room. Just as we got there—"Hup! Hup!"—Mr. Wexler rounded everybody up. "Time to go back to class, class!"

Our ultimate field trip was over.

Frankie and I formed a line with the other kids who had only been looking at books and hadn't been in one.

"That was a close call," Frankie said. "Do you think Mrs. Figglehopper knows? About the gates, I mean?"

"I'm not sure," I whispered. "But we definitely have to keep an eye on her. If she had really gotten them repaired, we might still be in 1872."

"Back to class," Mr. Wexler said as we filed into the hallway outside. "Excuse me, Devin, what is that?"

He pointed at my hand. I looked down. I still had the book. "Dude! I'm holding a . . . a . . . book!"

"Indeed!" said Mr. Wexler. "Please return it."

I ran back inside and set the book back on the stand. Frankie put the watch back, too. Together, we read the last page once more. Then we closed the book.

"One awesome story," I said.

"Definitely one of the best," she said. "We did so much stuff in there. Lots of excitement and danger."

140

"Passepartout was fun," I said. "Mr. Fogg was pretty cool and calm through the whole thing, though."

"He didn't do much sight-seeing," she said. "Plus, he spent a ton of money and brought back no souvenirs."

"He found Aouda," I said.

She grinned. "Yeah, he found Aouda. For a friend like that, I guess I'd make a trip around the world."

"Me, too," I said. "A couple of times, even."

She chuckled. "It makes me want to get some T-shirts made up. Frankie and Devin—the World Tour!"

"I love it! Except it should be Devin and Frankie—"

"And you know," she said, "I think we're getting pretty good at this reading thing. If we ever read *Around the World in Eighty Days* again, with what we know now I bet we could shave a day or two off Fogg's record."

I stared at her. "Whoa! Is that a bet?"

Frankie grinned at me. "You bet it's a bet!"

"You're on!"

With a laugh, we shook hands on it, then raced off down the hall to join our class.

Dear Reader:

Don't you just love to travel? Well, I do. And I've found no easier way to travel than by cozying up with a good classic book.

Around the World in Eighty Days is a delightful and funny book written by Jules Verne, who was born in Nantes, France, in 1828. As a young man, Jules studied law with the idea of taking over his father's practice. Instead, Jules surprised everyone by deciding to become a writer. He then spent several years trying to write hit plays.

Alas, his plays were failures.

But true inspiration was just around the corner!

Happening to meet the famous author Alexandre Dumas (who wrote *The Three Musketeers* and *The Count of Monte Cristo*, among other books), Jules declared, "If you are the great chronicler of history, I shall become the great chronicler of geography!"

And if you think about it, that's exactly what he did. His first book, *Five Weeks in a Balloon*, published in 1863, became quite successful. Following this, he wrote *Journey to the Center of the Earth* (1864), *From the Earth to the Moon* (1865), *Twenty Thousand Leagues Under the Sea* (1870), and *The Mysterious Island* (1874). In all these books, Jules takes his readers on extraordinary voyages in and around our world and those of the imagination.

He was influenced by the British novelist Charles Dickens and the American writer Edgar Allan Poe, but most people acknowledge that Jules practically invented what we now call science fiction. Even today, he is known as "the founding father of science fiction."

Jules was a hard worker all his life. By the time he died in 1905, he had written more than sixty novels.

His most popular is *Around the World in Eighty Days* (1873). When he wrote it, the era of speedy steamships and trains was approaching. Jules decided it would be fun to take some characters on a tour around the world, using all the quickest ways of getting from here to there.

What a fun journey! And what fun characters! I just love the emotional and lively Passepartout! Compare him to the cool and unflappable Phileas Fogg. Can you imagine two more opposite traveling companions?

Jules loved to write about geography and about worlds real or imagined, but his chief love was his characters. Even icy Phileas Fogg turns out to be quite lovable in the end. He is certainly a traveler in a hurry!

And speaking of being in a hurry, I must hurry. I have another class arriving in exactly—oh!—eighty seconds!

Note to self: Get Devin and Frankie to clean up the doughnut powder in the workroom.

Well, until next time—see you where the books are!

I. M. Figglehopper

Crack open the next book and take a peek at

#4: Humbug Holiday
(A Christmas Carol)

Chapter 1

"Hilli-ho, Devin!" a voice called out as I crashed through the front doors of Palmdale Middle School and tramped into the cafeteria.

"Yo-ho, there, Frankie!" the voice chirped when my best-friend-forever-despite-the-fact-that-she's-a-girl Frankie Lang breezed into the caf alongside me.

Frankie and I screeched to a stop.

The chirpy voice belonged to Mr. Wexler, our English teacher. he came trotting toward us now, a huge grin on his face and his wispy hair flying up behind him.

"Warning, warning," I said. "Mr. Wexler smiling. We have suddenly entered an alternate dimension of weirdness!"

Frankie chuckled. "Or maybe it's just good old Christmas spirit. After all, it's only two days until the big day."

"Which translates to—the last day of school before vacation!" I added.

"Well, well!" Mr. Wexler said, his face still beaming. "What do you think? Pretty wonderful, isn't it?"

He waved his arm around the cafeteria as if he were swishing an invisible cape.

The place was jammed with kids from our English class, taping red and green streamers to the ceiling, stringing twinkly white lights around the fake-frosted windows, decorating a Christmas tree, and piling up holiday baked goods on a couple of long tables.

"All this, just for us?" I said. "I feel honored. . . ."

Mr. Wexler laughted. "Ha! Good one, Devin. Now, really. What have you two brought in today, hmm?"

"Just ourselves, for a great day at school!" Frankie said, her smile twinkling like those Christmas lights.

"A great *last* day of school," I said, just because it sounded so good.

But as cheery as Frankie and I were getting, our teacher wasn't. He pointed up to a huge banner hanging over our heads. It read:

6TH-GRADE COMMUNITY CHRISTMAS BANQUET
FOOD DONATIONS DUE—TODAY!

"You do know our Christmas Banquet is today, don't you?" he asked. "We're hosting the Palmdale Homeless Shelter. You were supposed to bring in food for the charity dinner. You knew about this."

I blinked at the guy. "Are you sure we knew about this? Because my brain tells me we sort of didn't."

"You should have known about it," he replied. "We've talked about it for the last month in class—"

"Oh, in class!" said Frankie. Then she turned to me and whispered. "There's the problem, Devin. You were probably snoring too loud for me to hear."

I grumbled at my friend. "I don't snore. I sleep quite soundly, thank you—"

"We've talked about how there are families, even in sunny Palmdale, who don't eat as well as we do," Mr. Wexler went on. "Some people—children like yourselves—don't have as many clothes as we do."

"That's not good," I said.

"Hundreds of people in our town don't have proper food or shelter," our teacher said. "Our Christmas Banquet is just one way to help. It's part of the book project we're working on. Remember?"

Frankie frowned. "I guess we forgot to remember."

"Or maybe we remembered to forget," I said.

A huge sigh came from our teacher. "So, you didn't bring in food. Did you at least read the book?"

We stared at our teacher.

One thing you have to realize about Frankie and me is that as bad as we are about remembering (or even hearing) about school stuff, we're probably worse at the whole reading thing.

People say we don't read well because we fail to grasp that we're actually supposed to open the books, not just carry them around.

I say it's because they cram too many words in books, and make you read all of the words, or it doesn't count.

"Do you even *have* the book?" Mr. Wexler asked, setting his hands on his hips in that out-of-patience way he has. "You both have backpacks. Are they empty?"

"Of course not!" Frankie scoffed. She tipped her backpack over. A hairbrush fell out. "Now, it's empty."

Mr. Wexler grumbled, then turned to me. "Devin?"

"Mine's not empty, but it sure isn't crammed with books!" I said.

Narrowing his eyes, Mr. Wexler stepped over to a table, picked up a thin book, and held it up in front of us. "It's called *A Christmas Carol*. Jog any memories?"

"Wait a second," I said. "I know this book. Isn't it all about a girl named Carol wo wears red and green at the same time?"

"That's right," said Frankie. "Even though red and green together is a way tremendous fashion risk. I heard about that book, too. Wasn't there a movie—"

"Not even close," Mr. Wexler cut in, wrinkling his eyebrows. Or, I should say eye*brow*, since he really only has one. It stretches over both eyes, is very bushy, and wiggles like a fuzzy black caterpillar when he gets mad.

It was wiggling now.

He shook his head at me. "Frankly, I expected much better things. . . ."

"No, I'm Devin. She's Frankly," I said.

I was joking. But actually we both knew why Mr. Wexler expected better things from us. You see, even though we find it tough to read, Frankie and I have actually gotten good grades in Mr. Wexler's English class. How, you ask?

I'll tell you, I say!

In a single word—the zapper gates.

That's three words, Frankie would say, because she's such a math whiz.

What are the zapper gates, you ask?

I will tell you that, too.

The zapper gates are these old, supposedly busted security gates that our school librarian, Mrs. Figglehopper, keeps in the library workroom. But—as Frankie and I have found out—those gates are anything but busted.

They are the most amazing—and secret—things

5

ever. What happens when you get near them is—

Wait, I'll tell you later. Mr. Wexler is talking again.

"Perhaps you'd both better just report to the library," he said. "I'm sure Mrs. Figglehopper will find a copy of the book for you to read!"

"But if we go to the library, we'll miss the beginning of the banquet," I protested.

"And while you're there," he continued, "maybe you can think about how important this event is to everyone—and why it should be important to you, too."

"But, Mr. Wexler, there's food here. And we love food," Frankie pleaded. "Do we have to go right now?"

He gave us the eyebrow.

We went right then.